Praise for
Jackie Tempo and the Emperor's Seal

"Suzanne Litrel shows why her armload of awards as a Social Studies teacher is well earned. Combining an intriguing time-travel plot, the travails of typical [and some not-so-typical] young adults and a wealth of historical information, *Jackie Tempo and The Emperor's Seal* fully achieves the elusive goal of informing while entertaining by truly putting the "story" into its history."

—Steve Corso
Lead Social Studies Teacher, Advanced Placement Instructor
John Glenn High School
Long Island, New York

"I find [Jackie Tempo] to be an exciting novel that gives insight to ancient Chinese culture and ideals. The vocabulary makes the characters almost alive."

—Michael Stern, 8th grade

Jackie Tempo and the Emperor's Seal

Jackie Tempo and the Emperor's Seal

Suzanne Litrel

December
2008

Dear Rebecca —

enjoy your

"travels" through

China!

[signature]

iUniverse, Inc.
New York Lincoln Shanghai

Jackie Tempo and the Emperor's Seal

Copyright © 2007 by Suzanne M. Litrel

iUniverse books may be ordered through booksellers or by contacting:

iUniverse
2021 Pine Lake Road, Suite 100
Lincoln, NE 68512
www.iuniverse.com
1-800-Authors (1-800-288-4677)

Because of the dynamic nature of the Internet, any Web addresses or links contained in this book may have changed since publication and may no longer be valid.

This is a work of fiction. All of the characters, names, incidents, organizations, and dialogue in this novel are either the products of the author's imagination or are used fictitiously.

ISBN: 978-0-595-46822-5 (pbk)
ISBN: 978-0-595-91112-7 (ebk)

Printed in the United States of America

This book is dedicated to my mother

Judith Anne Aubrey Segalini

who traveled many lifetimes in one.

Acknowledgements

First and foremost, I'd like to thank the students of Bay Shore High School. You have taught me that a good story is worth the telling and brings history to life. Thank you for your good humor, shining intelligence, and boundless creative energy. I must also express my deep appreciation for the staff of Bay Shore schools. You are dedicated visionaries, and it's my honor to serve with you.

My friends and family have been wonderfully supportive of the Jackie Tempo series. In particular, the following people have long suffered the story of a time-travelling teen in search of her parents, and you have only ever given me complete and unconditional support. Thank you for your unrelenting enthusiasm: Jessica Durrie, Isobel Shih, Ann Litrel, Judy Farabaugh, Anthony J. Gallo, Gloria Sesso, Joe Nardi, Pat and Bob Ponzi, Ursula Limpert, Heather Thompson, Walter Fishon, John Selzer, Matt Pasca and Terri Muuss, Nell Kalter, and also my sisters Deborah Kloosterman and Carolyn Segalini. My father lent an editorial eye as well.

I'd also like to acknowledge the enthusiasm and expertise of my editor Karen Schader and my website designer Kathleen Lukachinski. I am in awe of your talent. Thank you for bringing Jackie Tempo to life.

Thanks also go to my son Alec and daughter Julia, both of whom have endured countless readings of Jackie Tempo at the dinner table. Your enthusiasm has buoyed me even as I wondered whether to come up with more palatable meals.

Finally, to my husband Christopher, who told me to quit talking and start writing: I can't imagine, not for one second, a more supportive partner. We have traveled so far together—from the University of Michigan to Taiwan and China, through Eastern Europe during the waning days of the Cold War and finally to New York. Yet even as we journey on this wonderful path called parenthood, you have always urged me to follow through on all my dreams. Thank you.

Contents

We live, not as we wish to, but as we can.

Mencius

CHAPTER 1

▼

LOST IN PARADISE

"No one can touch this book but you. Ever."

A commanding voice pierced the late-afternoon gloom of the mahogany-paneled library. High on a book ladder, a short, stout woman blew the dust off a heavy, leather-bound tome and held it out to a girl who waited below. The woman wore a floor-length, black silk robe with a high Mandarin collar, and for a moment it seemed as if she might trip over its hem, but she gripped the ladder rails and stepped nimbly down.

The girl, a slight fifteen-year-old with long, curly auburn hair, sagged under the weight of the old book and exchanged curious glances with the dark-haired young man who stood nearby. A whorl of dust tickled her nose and she turned her head to sneeze; he sneezed as well.

The woman's purple eyes gleamed in the lamplight, as did her brilliant white hair, done up high in elaborate coils. Her velvet-slippered feet whispered against the floor as she drew close to the pair. "Careful ... CARE ... FUL!" She steered the girl to a richly patterned velvet sofa. The boy followed. "Now ... SIT! I will explain how this book works."

Aunt Isobel was the only family Jackie had. Just a few months ago, Jackie's parents had died in a car crash. With no other living relatives, it had fallen to the eccentric but enormously wealthy woman to raise Jackie, the daughter of her younger sister.

Suiting her dramatic style of dress, Aunt Isobel was a woman of grand pronouncements and gestures. While she had tried, for Jackie's sake, to stick with her idea of a typical family routine, three square meals a day and all, she simply chafed at the pretense of order. A dealer in expensive art and antiques, she needed the thrill of the unexpected, the excitement of the chase after fine objects. The intrigue of the art world fascinated her. From Jackie's first week at the house, her aunt had jetted off to Singapore and Venice for strange excursions from which she'd spend a full day recovering. Later, dark trucks would roll up to the service entrance of the grand old house, and mysterious crates would be unloaded and stored in its back wing.

Jackie didn't care. She didn't mind being left in the stately mansion. The kids at her new school loved to whisper that there were ghosts lurking in the cobwebs of Shangri-La, as the house was called. "She probably even talks with the dead," one mean girl sneered. "She sure can't communicate with the living." *Good,* she had thought then. *Maybe I'll get to see my parents.* And with that thought she had choked up and turned away from the nasty classmate. Indeed, she'd rather hang out with ghosts than with most of the people she'd met at Arborville High.

In fact, most of the kids Jackie had met at the new school were horrible, though she'd had hopes for the place when she first saw the building. With its grand steps leading up to impressive double doors, it was certainly nicer looking than her old high school, which, she had to admit, looked a bit like a shoebox by comparison. More overwhelming than the architecture, however, were the well-established cliques. On her first day, no one had acknowledged her presence, except for her history teacher. "Class, we have a student who is new to Arborville," Ms. Thompson had said. "It's not easy to switch schools in the middle of the semester, so be sure to welcome her." The other kids all turned to stare at Jackie—and then proceeded to ignore her for the next few months.

But Jackie didn't feel much like socializing, anyway. The week of her parents' death had been a blur; the funeral was hastily put together by her parents' friends, and then Aunt Isobel, whom Jackie had met only once before, swooped in and took her away. Jackie had packed her favorite books, stuffed animals, and a suitcase of clothes and soon found herself in Arborville, a small New England town on a peninsula that stretched a few miles out into the ocean.

Aunt Isobel had poked around the Tempos' small house the day after the funeral. "We will see that your house is properly packed up, and that your possessions are sent to us. But … must you take your … dog with you?" She had looked at Wolfe, Jackie's massive black Labrador, with obvious distaste. "I have a lovely cat, you know."

Jackie was not so shell-shocked by her parents' death that she couldn't protest. "I'm not going anywhere without Wolfe," she had said, dropping to her knees and burying her face in his warm neck. It was settled, then. Aunt Isobel had bundled them all into her limousine late that night, never, it seemed, to return.

True to Aunt Isobel's word, Jackie's family furniture and paintings had arrived at Shangri-La not a scant ten days later. The mansion lived up to its namesake: it was set in a remote, fairly inaccessible part of town, but with a breathtakingly beautiful view of the craggy countryside and ocean. Clearly, this was a paradise of sorts.

Not now. Now she felt lost; she might as well have been stuck in the Himalayas like the fictional Shangri-La. *Whatever*, she had thought dully, as she watched all her stuff get unloaded and placed in the Green Wing, which was nearly as big as her family's whole house.

"Whatever," she said out loud. The word fit everything she was feeling.

"There!" Aunt Isobel had exclaimed as a worn and familiar sofa was set in front of Jackie's very own fireplace, in her very own drawing room. "What a delight—the gift of independence!" She had peered over the rims of her rhinestone-studded glasses. "Isn't it true that all teens need is a space of their own? Well then, I'm right next door, in the Blue Wing. Make yourself at home. Oh, and"—she patted Jackie's arm—"it's so, er, totally cool to have you here."

Jackie winced at her aunt's social efforts. She slid away from Isobel and forced a smile.

"Thanks," she said. "I agree."

But of course Jackie didn't feel at home—not without her mom and dad. She had traveled widely with her parents, both university professors, and had learned that home was wherever one's family chose to stay: a hotel, an apartment, even a houseboat. But not this forbidding mansion atop a remote bluff overlooking the gray Atlantic. Aunt Isobel came and went like a summer storm, sudden and dramatic. Except for Dona Marta, the Brazilian housekeeper, Jackie was usually alone with Wolfe in the mansion. All alone.

And so Jackie and Wolfe took to spending the afternoons roaming the mansion and its English gardens, following the set paths to nowhere and starting over again. Toward evening, she'd head to Shangri-La's huge granite and marble kitchen, where Dona Marta would be swaying to soft Brazilian music as she prepared dinner. "*Venha ca, querida,*" she'd call in a lilting voice, as she tossed a fresh salad, picked right from the garden outside the kitchen door. "Come to dinner, my dear." Aunt Isobel traveled most weeks, and even when she was home, she kept eccentric hours and mealtimes. So Jackie was on her own. Still, Aunt Isobel had instructed Dona Marta to stick to "normal" mealtimes for her niece, even if not for herself.

That all changed the day she announced her trip to Katmandu.

If I have even a little sense, I will walk on the main road,
and my only fear will be of straying from it.
Keeping to the main road is easy,
but people love to be sidetracked.
Lao-tzu

CHAPTER 2

▼

THE SECRETS OF SAMARKAND

One blustery afternoon in early spring, driving rain assaulted Shangri-La and a furious wind whipped the gardens. But deep inside, the mansion was an oasis of calm. Jackie nestled in the library's window seat, partially hidden by the lush velvet drapes. Wolfe slept fitfully at her feet, dreaming, perhaps, of having to go outside in such atrocious weather.

For all the luxury of the Green Wing, it was here in the old library that Jackie felt at home. Three walls had ceiling-to-floor books of every genre from science fiction to ancient history; the fourth wall was distinguished by deep windows set over bookshelves. Between the windows, a pair of grand French doors opened to a slate terrace that hung over a bluff. Jackie's view of the rough Atlantic below was unobstructed.

She hugged her thin knees to her chest. Any moment now, Dona Marta would find her here, in the usual spot, and scold her for skipping lunch. Not that she had much of an appetite for anything these days. She pressed her cheek against the cold windowpane and stared out at the storm. A large tree limb hurtled over the terrace wall and into the ocean. *That's me,* Jackie thought dully. *No control ... just here for the ride.*

Wolfe shifted uneasily and whined. Jackie reached down to pet her only friend and then slid down to join him on the thick Persian carpet whose patterns covered much of the room.

Her eyes filled with tears as she remembered the last great storm she had been in, the storm that had robbed her of her parents as their car slid off a slick highway, minutes away from home. Only Jackie had survived, and she remembered nothing of the crash except for the spinning of the car and a blinding, white explosion.

And now she was here. In some stupid hotel of a house, Shangri-La, which was anything but a paradise.

"Jacqueline?" Aunt Isobel's voice shattered Jackie's dark thoughts. "JACQUELINE? Oh, JAC-QUE-LINE?"

"Here, I'm here, Aunt Isobel." Jackie peeled herself off the rug, wincing at the formal use of her name. Wolfe snorted, opened an eye, and rested his large head on her foot.

"Where? Oh ... yes, how can I miss that hair, even in this dark room!" Aunt Isobel exclaimed, as she swept into the room and switched on a Tiffany floor lamp. The stained-glass lampshade bathed the room in a soft, eerie light. "There, that's much better." She raised one eyebrow—just one—and glanced at her niece. "Weren't you wearing the same outfit yesterday?"

Jackie looked down. Her aunt was right. It was late Sunday morning, and she'd not only slept in these baggy jeans and sweater, but all she'd done since waking up was brush her teeth and pull her hair into a ragged ponytail. Not that it mattered much. *Whatever.*

"Tsk, what a shame. With your beauty ..." She fixed on Jackie's green eyes and reached up to pat her hair, then gave her niece a quick but suffocating hug. And just as quickly, she was all business again. "Well, then. I am packing for an art excursion in Katmandu, although I'm terribly afraid that the place has been pillaged by Westerners before me."

"But aren't you a Westerner too?" Jackie couldn't help herself.

"Dear, dear!" Aunt Isobel glared. "The operative word here is *pillaged!*" She thrust a piece of paper under Jackie's nose. "Which is exactly what has happened to your world history grades! Shocking—and absolutely unacceptable!" She waved the terrible report card in her niece's face. "The daughter of two history professors failing out of school! I won't have it!" Her face softened. "Judith and I were inseparable. I can't fail my sister now."

Good luck, lady. Jackie flushed with sudden anger at the mention of her mother's name. How much could her aunt care about her schoolwork, anyway? She was never really around.

"I daresay you've been moping and whiling away your days, and that's just not healthy or productive—especially for a young girl like you! So …"—Aunt Isobel's eyes gleamed—"I'd like to introduce you to your new world history tutor!" She turned toward the library entrance. "Jon, please come in, now!" she trilled.

A handsome, lanky boy sauntered into the grand library, backpack in hand. He whistled as he surveyed row upon row of books. "Wow," he said, pushing a handful of shaggy, dark hair out of his eyes. "Nasty!"

"I beg your pardon?" Aunt Isobel stiffened.

"I mean, this is way cool. Whoa!" Jon Durrie leaned over a glass table that held a very old map. "This looks like an original Mercator projection!"

Aunt Isobel beamed. "You've a fine eye, appearances to the contrary." She grimaced as she took in his baggy pants, belted low, and his T-shirt, which read "*I didn't do it!*"

She turned to her niece. "Jacqueline, dearest, Jon is going to help you write your history paper while I'm away. Now shake hands," she ordered.

Jackie had seen this guy around school. He was a junior, she knew that much about him, and he seemed to get along with everyone. *And no wonder*, she thought. He was cute, really cute—strong jaw, broad shoulders, dark blue eyes brightening his pale face.

She was nervous. It figured that the only way she'd get to talk to Mr. Popular here was if her rich aunt paid him. Still, she stuck out her hand. "You can call me Jackie, if you want," she mumbled to the floor.

"Oh, Jacqueline, please!" Aunt Isobel cried. "I never did get used to that dreadful nickname!" Jackie glowered at her aunt; hearing her full name always made her feel like she was in trouble. Jon looked away.

"Um, ma'am," he inquired politely, "didn't you say you had some resources on the topic of Chinese exploration during the Ming Dynasty? We can start with those." He turned to Jackie. "That's the paper topic, right? I had Ms. Thompson, too, and she's a tough grader. I'll show you what to do."

Jackie nodded dumbly, barely able to focus on his words. This was the worst. He was way too popular with the in crowd at school and would probably make fun of her behind her back. How ever would she be able to work with him?

It was at this point that Aunt Isobel had climbed the book ladder and retrieved the musty volume that made both Jon and Jackie sneeze.

When they were both seated, Aunt Isobel continued in a solemn tone. "Everything you need is in this book. It is priceless. It came from Samarkand, eleventh century perhaps … and I never could part with it."

Jackie glanced up at her aunt and raised an eyebrow. "Some old book from who-knows-where is going to help me write a paper about China? C'mon!" She felt anxious and frustrated. The paper was due next week.

Aunt Isobel seemed to shrink in the book's presence. "There are several things you need to know about this powerful ." She reached for it. "Hand it over. Now."

From the depths of the sofa, Jackie fingered the worn binding and curious, intricate design on the cover. She traced the swirling designs with her index finger and was surprised to find herself lulled by the movement.

Jon leaned over to see. "Cool, way cool."

Then Jackie opened the book.

"Stop!" Aunt Isobel cried.

At once Jackie was overcome by the strong scent of jasmine, and she closed her eyes as she inhaled the dizzyingly rich aroma. As if from a great distance, she heard her aunt say, "Ah, sixteenth century. I should have known. A time of great upheaval, to be sure." Her eyes open now, she strained to see in the unnatural darkness.

"Aunt Isobel! Where are you?" she called out, barely able to hear herself above the din of what seemed to be a thousand beating drums. She reached out for her aunt, but found only thin air.

"Jacqueline ... Jacqueline ... whatever you do ..."—she could barely hear her aunt now—"hold on to the book ... never let it go ..." Aunt Isobel's voice was fading by the second. "Follow the Middle Road home ..."

Jackie was spinning now, faster and faster, and for a second she seemed to hover above the sofa, where she saw her own slumped form, book spread across her lap, Aunt Isobel kneeling beside her, leaning forward and clasping her hands. Jon was gone.

The darkness broke over her again. A sudden whirring, and then all was still.

Life is really simple, but we insist on
making it complicated.
Confucius

C H A P T E R 3

▼

THE START OF A
REALLY LONG DAY

"I told you—this is no place for a young wench!" Jackie opened her eyes slowly. She turned towards the voice, wincing. Her head ached fiercely. Even the soft light of the oil lantern proved too much for her.

"And as I told you, sir—I had no idea she was on board!" Jackie's eyes flew open, and she struggled to sit up. It was her father, holding a lantern and peering anxiously at her.

"Daddy …?" She rubbed her eyes. "Where am I? What happened?" They were in what seemed to be a small wood compartment. The two men took up the entire space of the room. The only light emanated from the lantern. She felt queasy; the room was swaying. And she herself was swaying, too—in a hammock! She reached for her father.

"There, there," he murmured, drawing her to his strong chest. "You took a fall, and hit your head, but ye'll be fine soon enough."

"Oh, Daddy." She'd missed him so much. His linen shirt, stiff from many a saltwater washing, scratched her face. She pulled back. There was her father, all right, but in what appeared to be quite old-fashioned clothing! He wore a long-sleeved, white linen shirt and high-waisted dark pants, and he clutched a top hat in his hands. She looked down and noted his dark boots. His thick blond hair was pulled back in a loose ponytail, and his handsome face was framed by mutton-chop whiskers.

This couldn't be. Her father, a university professor, always wore jeans. He had short hair and was clean-shaven. She rubbed her eyes. "Daddy? I don't understand …?"

"Aye, that makes two of us, wench! And as for you, Tempo, you bloody dago," the burly captain stomped his foot, "this'll be yer last trip on my vessel, d'ye hear! You and yer daughter," he spat out the word, "can find yer own ways back!" and he stormed out, cursing to

himself. Every sailor knew it was terrible luck to have a
female on ship. "Women! They'll always sneak behind
yer back!"

David Tempo grinned at his daughter. "You're
looking good, kid." He hugged her again. "But up you
go. We've got to get going." He pulled her gently out
of the hammock. Jackie gave a little hop to the floor.

"Oh!" She stumbled as her high-laced black boots
hit the floor and snagged on her muslin dress. "What
the—!" Her hand flew up to her head. Her thick red
hair was knotted loosely at the nape of her neck. She
looked up at her father in puzzlement.

"Come, come," he said, grasping her hand. "You'll
get used to all that soon enough. I'll explain later."
They left his dank cabin, and were almost immediately
accosted by a swarthy crewmate.

His sour breath nearly overpowered Jackie, who by
now was feeling ever more faint, and not just because
of the injury to her head. There was no room to
maneuver in the narrow corridor. She stepped back-
wards into her cabin, stepping on her father's toes.

'G'day." The man grinned, revealing three missing
teeth. "Name's Jenkins. I haven't had the pleasure
of—"

Jackie's father pulled her behind him.

"Jenkins," he said sternly, "back to your post, or—" he said slyly, staring straight into the sailor's eyes, "do I have to check on the steward's supply of rum?"

Jenkins backed down the corridor, hat in hand. "Nay, doctor." He disappeared.

By now, Jackie was feeling downright claustrophobic. "Dad, I'm itching to get out of here!" She pushed him forward.

"Itching? Really?" David Tempo ran a calloused hand through her hair. "Let me see!"

"No, Dad, c'mon!" Jackie grabbed his hand and stared at it.

His was not the soft, pale hand of an intellectual. She ran her fingers slowly over his scabbed and hardened palm. His skin was so dry it was cracked between several fingers.

Jackie thought back to the long winter evenings she would spend with her parents in the parlor of their restored colonial home. Her mother used to look for meaning in their hands. She would point out curious features of their heart and head, or career, lines. "All's well, there, I suppose," she had said wryly, the firelight warming her delicate features. "Looks like we'll all have stellar careers. But," she had continued, amber locks escaping from a loose-knit twist held at the nape of her neck, "we all have the same strange break in our life lines." She had glanced up quickly, then, locking eyes with her husband. "We all seem to have two life lines, almost as if we would live parallel lives." Her gaze fell upon young Jackie. "All of us."

Jackie had thought nothing of it then, of course, as she basked in the love of her parents, sketching as they read, eventually falling asleep to their discussions on Descartes, Plato, and the quirks of the time-space continuum. But she thought back to that night now, as she peered into her father's palm, unable to make out his life, heart or head lines for all the scarring in his hand.

"Aye, life on the seas is not easy on the hands," David Tempo said ruefully, drawing his daughter close. She wondered if he thought back to that same evening, too.

But there was no more time for reflection or regrets.

An alarm was raised, a deafening bell that brought Jackie's hands to her ears. She could hear shouting, above, and the heavy tread of sailors manning their stations.

"Now we have to get out of here," Jackie's father said. Sailors ran past his door, urgent and intense. "We're being boarded, and not for a customs inspection, it seems." He thrust some clothes at her, "Put these on." For once, he was fearful.

Jackie had enough. She crossed her arms. "No," she said stubbornly, "this is all a dream. Wake up." She shook her head. "Wake up, up, up!"

Her father pinched her—hard. Jackie yelped and rubbed her arm in surprise.

"Dream enough for you?" His eyes flashed. "It's 1521. We're on a Portuguese caravel. We're off the coast of southern China. The Chinese are not happy that we're here. And the waters are full of Japanese pirates, far from home, ready to loot any ship they can. Now—move it!" Jackie nodded dumbly and grabbed the clothes. Her eyes smarted with tears. Her father had never been that rough on her before.

David Tempo turned his back on her to block the door and keep lookout. "God help us if they find out you're a woman."

Jackie was not interested in finding out who *they* were. She did as she was told, tucking her long hair into her sailor's cap. Fortunately, she was of wiry, athletic build, honed from years of training in the martial arts. She willed herself into action, even as her fingers shook. It took three attempts to pull the drawstring of her sailor's pants tight.

Then she tapped her father's shoulder. "Ready." Her voice was clear and strong. Her father handed her a small satchel. Jackie slung it across her shoulders without a word. David Tempo smiled grimly down at her and held her hand.

"Let's go."

The scene above deck was even more confusing than that below. Sailors ran back and forth, alternately cursing, shouting, and praying. Jackie clutched her father's hand. He held it tight.

"Ye'd better be prepared to meet the Maker!" An old shiphand rolled his eyes in fear and grabbed at them. He was sweating profusely beneath his long striped cap. "They'll be boarding any minute now!" He pointed up. "Look!"

For once, Jackie's father was at a loss for words. He gaped at the large vessel that had drawn up alongside their proud caravel. It soared above their sturdy ship, which had voyaged more than one thousand miles from the port of Lisbon. High above the square, rotating sails, above the tallest of the three masts, rose a Chinese treasure ship, easily seven times the size of theirs. The Chinese ship looked to be over four hundred feet long; its nine grand masts rendered the Portuguese ship toy-like. Nonetheless, it was clearly capable of maneuvering into aggressive action, and it was doing so now.

"Well I'll be damned," Tempo whistled. "Chinese treasure ships! Even so many years after the death of the mighty explorer Zheng He!"

"We'll all be damned!" the old man cried. "Look!"

Suddenly, a dozen grappling hooks whirred over and onto the main deck of the caravel, and the Portuguese sailors could only jump back defensively as the ships pulled tight together. Jackie clung to her father as dozens of fierce Chinese sailors poured on board. They were brandishing swords!

David pulled his daughter away and grabbed her shoulders tight. He pulled her to him.

"I'm not ready to lose you again … not just yet," he whispered hoarsely. For all the bedlam, Jackie could only fix on her father's steely eyes. "We'll jump, then."

She nodded. After all, she could swim. It was the only way off the ship, which was burning by now. As they drew near the side, she heard a groan.

"Wait!" She pulled her father towards the sound. There, flat under the ropes, was Jon Durrie! There was no time to waste. She reached out towards him.

"Come," she pleaded. Jackie gave him her hand.

He was rigid with shock; a bruise darkened his left cheek.

"Let's go, young man." Professor Tempo dragged him out, hands under his armpits. Jon stumbled to his feet and stared at the two. "Can ye swim, son?" Jon nodded. *Yes.*

David Tempo sighed. "This won't be easy." He grabbed Jackie's upper arm with his left hand, Jon with his right. Then he dashed forward and dragged them up and over the railing.

And over they jumped, all three.

And remember, no matter where you go, there you are.
Confucius

CHAPTER 4

▼

THIS IS NOT A DREAM … UNFORTUNATELY

Jackie surfaced first, gasping for air. She sputtered and pushed away from the doomed caravel. The water was surprisingly warm.

"Da—" she shouted, flailing about.

With a great crash, the top half of the main mast fell burning into the water. Jackie narrowly avoided being struck.

"DADDY!" This time she shrieked at the top of her lungs. She didn't care who heard her. She smacked the water in frustration. Men were jumping overboard, now, heedless of the fact that they couldn't swim. They were trying to avoid a worse fate—that of being burned alive or hacked to pieces.

She turned her face up to the sky, sunset-streaked now, its warm colors reflecting the turmoil and confusion below, in what she decided was the South China Sea.

"Help me, oh angel of mercy!" A drowning sailor clutched at her, dragging her down into the waters with him.

Then all went dark.

She first felt, rather than saw, the tightly packed grains of sand pressing into her right cheek. Her mouth was slightly open, and a thin line of spittle trickled out. She was curled into a fetal position, arms crossing her chest, one foot bare. She felt stiff, as if she'd been in this position for days; she couldn't tell. The surf pounded the beach, no more than ten feet from where she lay curled.

Then she heard a sharp crack, followed by the acrid smell of smoke. Jackie forced her eyes open. She could barely make out a thin, ragged figure squatting on its haunches, poking at the fire. The figure glanced at her sharply, but she couldn't make out any features; it was too dark out. Jackie lapsed into unconsciousness again.

Now the sun beat down on her bare foot; the rest of her was in shade. A palm tree bowed over her like a ballerina in a deep curtsey, gracefully blocking the sun with its thick fronds.

She had been dragged some way up the beach, judging from the soreness under her arms. It was very hot out; she had perspired through her garments. Flat on her back, Jackie stretched, extending her limbs out as far as they could go. Then, with a deep breath, she pushed herself up, first to her elbows, then, with another sharp inhalation, to a sitting position. She felt bruised all over; it hurt to even breathe.

Jackie stared down at her half-clad feet in bemusement. The naked foot, pinkened by the harsh sun, looked small and worn, as if it had walked a thousand miles. She wriggled her toes. On her other foot was a wrinkled stocking and a leather shoe fastened by a dull silver buckle. She looked down at herself. Yes, she was dressed in mid-sixteenth century sailor's garb. She pulled at a twisted strand of reddish hair. Her arm hurt, and she remembered her father's harsh pinch. Yes, as far as she could tell, she was still Jackie Tempo.

On a beach. Somewhere in China. Thousands of miles and more than four hundred years from home.

The journey of a thousand miles begins with a single step.
Lao-tzu

C H A P T E R   5

▼

THE RUNAWAY

How had it come to this? Jackie shifted and felt a stiff, square object digging into her back. She stood up and reached around; it was something in the satchel her father had given her, just before they'd jumped off the ship. Jackie pulled it out the offending object. It looked like some sort of journal, leather bound, with a clasp in front. For all her recent mishaps, the volume looked unharmed.

Aunt Isobel's book! Jackie scrambled to undo the clasp, but it was stuck. Her fingers trembled with excitement—and not a little bit of fear.

"C'mon, c'mon," she muttered. Just as she was about to lose hope, the clasp gave and the pages fluttered with a crackling energy. She detected a faint smell of ashes and perfume.

The book opened to a map of China that was marked by a score of Chinese characters. Jackie noticed a road that snaked its way northward through apparently rugged terrain.

"From the South China Sea," she read, "take the High Road north. This will lead you to the Middle Road. From there, you will find the Gateway to the Next World, which you must enter without delay. Remember," she continued, "this is not a journey that you will take alone. Help comes from unexpected quarters." She tried to turn the page, but it was stuck.

"Oh!" Jackie drew a sharp breath and nearly dropped the book in surprise. A strange tingling sensation spiked through her fingers and then through her entire body. She was reading Chinese! She slammed the book shut. This was way too weird. *Dear God or whoever else is out there, let this nightmare end!* She scrunched her eyes shut and tried to will herself back to her aunt's library, where she had been having a cozy afternoon with Wolfe.

"Please, may I offer you tea?"

Jackie jumped. It was the ragged person from the evening before, but in the daylight she could see that it was a young woman, her shiny black hair in two long braids running down her back. Like Jackie, she was dressed as a man, but in torn peasant trousers with a tunic for a shirt. Her feet were bare. She was very pretty and looked quite young, perhaps no more than fourteen.

Jackie was definitely not back in Aunt Isobel's library.

"T-tea?" Jackie stuttered. Sweat trickled down her back. Maybe the sun had fried her brains. "You speak English?" she asked, feeling somewhat stupid. Obviously the young girl spoke English.

The girl nodded and held out a steaming cup of tea. Jackie reached for it with both hands, as the green ceramic cup had no handles. She hesitated before bringing the hot liquid to her lips.

The girl nodded once more. "Hot tea, to cool the body." She glanced quickly at Jackie's rumpled figure, and then down again at the sand.

As far as Jackie could tell, they were the only two living beings on earth. To the north, the coastline extended as far as she could strain her eyes, and was backed by dunes and dense shrubbery. The sea was as smooth as glass; sunlight glinted off its surface. *Perfect spring break spot,* Jackie thought ruefully. She stole a glance at her patient host. Spring break might not be a concept she would understand.

Just a short distance to the south, Jackie spotted a very busy trading port. Huge ships, like the nine-masted vessel she had seen the night before, lay anchored in the harbor, with smaller vessels moving busily around them. On this very calm day, men's voices carried clearly.

A loud cry went up, and Jackie saw that the contents of one of the great treasure ships were being discharged. Half-clad, well-muscled men in teams of four carried treasure chests; long ivory tusks were unloaded; and several types of animals were brought out from the deepest compartments of the elaborately designed ship. A great shout heralded the arrival of something unusual. Jackie squinted: a crowd had gathered on the shore. Just then, two stiff-legged giraffes were dragged out!

Jackie gasped in shock, but the girl merely smiled. "Yes, our treasure ships have brought back all manner of tribute to our land, including those from faraway regions. While we Chinese have been sailing the seas for many, many centuries, it was not until the great eunuch explorer Zheng He that our kingdom's maritime reach extended to other, very distant worlds."

What a weird conversation, Jackie thought. *I'll probably be dead by tomorrow and I'm talking about some eunuch with someone from another century.* She wondered how the girl came to speak English. "How is it that you speak my language?"

"I was taught to read and write English and Chinese by one of your own kind," said Mei Li. "A very nice man who in many ways resembles you, but not because you are both round-eyed, with pale skin and strange red hair. I first met him when I was quite young, and no one believed that I had such a strange-looking friend. But he is real, even if I haven't seen him for many weeks now. I called him Mr. Tai— he had a long, funny name which I could not pronounce—and his nose was much bigger than yours, which is not so big after all." Mei Li chattered quickly, a bit nervous at being so close up to the white foreigner.

"Tempo—was his name David Tempo?" Jackie interrupted, her anxiety and confusion getting in the way of her manners. The girl stared back at her, and shrugged. She couldn't remember; it was hard to keep foreign names straight. "What about a boy my age? There was a ship, I was on a burning ship, and …" Jackie sank down into the sand, sobbing.

It was just too much for her to bear. The downed ship, finding and losing her father, Jon lost here somewhere as well, where was her aunt, and could her mother possibly be alive, somewhere, anywhere in this confused universe? And the book! It was her way out, but she couldn't leave now, not without her father or Jon.

According to Aunt Isobel's instructions, Jackie had to look for a gateway if she were to find her way back to the twenty-first century. She squeezed her eyes shut. What gateway? Certainly there were none to be found on this beach. Was she to enter every door she saw? How would she know which one to pass through? Her mother had always taught her to trust her intuition. Well, right now her intuition was telling her ... nothing.

"Come, let us go." The Chinese girl tapped Jackie's shoulder. "I am Xie Mei Li. You may call me Mei Li, for that is my given name. As for my family name ..." she trailed off. It was not the time to think about her own family now; this barbarian girl needed her help. Besides, the girl reminded her of Mr. Tai, who used to be one of her friends.

"I'm Jacqueline Tempo." Jackie stuck out her hand. "But my friends call me Jackie for short." Mei Li stared at the outstretched hand. She knew that Westerners greet each other this way. Odd, how they pressed each other's palms, as if it were a ritual of the greatest importance. Still, she reached out too, and they shook hands.

Mei Li bent down to pack her few possessions in a bundle, which she then strapped to her back. She pointed to Jackie's remaining shoe.

"You should take it off, so as not to become unbalanced. I will get you a pair of sandals. Come,"—she held out her hand to the worn foreigner, the *waiguoren*—"let us go. Let us search for this man you speak of, Tempo." The two young women, both about same height, made their way up the beach together, and disappeared through the dense shrubbery that surrounded it.

You can not open a book without learning something.
Confucius

CHAPTER 6

▼

THE ROAD LESS TRAVELED

The two girls hid in a rice paddy until dusk. Then they stole along the narrow paths that carved through the irregularly shaped, wet plots, just after the last peasant filed home from a hard day's toil in the fields. Jackie followed Mei Li's certain steps as the last rays of sun glinted over the low-lying mountains.

"There!" Me Li had spotted something. She rolled her linen trousers up to her knees, waded out among the young rice shoots, and fished out a large triangular hat in triumph. "Put it on. It will hide your pale face."

The reed hat was wet, but Jackie was too tired and hungry to argue. They had been walking all day, stopping only once for tea and a small bowl of rice they stole from the kitchen of a large compound. This was just after midday, and everyone from the sentries at the gate to the peasants in the fields was taking an after-lunch nap. Thus it was that Mei Li, with a stealth that Jackie was beginning to admire, had taken two scoops of rice out from under the snoring cook's nose and ladled them into the ceramic bowl she carried in her ragged knapsack.

"*Hao*," Jackie assented and clamped the hat on. Though the evening was warm, she shivered as water dripped down her back. Still, for once, Mei Li did not correct her pronunciation; had she mastered one word of Chinese? Or perhaps her traveling companion was tired, too. Still, she could not contain her curiosity about her surroundings.

"Can rice really grow there, too?" Jackie pointed to the terraced hills. She had seen photos of these small hillside plots, but could hardly envision their beauty, up close. "And how do the peasants get up there, anyway?" Jackie pointed to a tiny plot at the top of a large hill, so high it seemed to scrape the heavens. Mei Li frowned up at the sky, and Jackie noticed that storm clouds were rolling in. They'd better find shelter, and fast.

"Questions, all the time questions," Mei Li grumbled as she trod steadily forward. "Why is it that foreigners make so much noise?" she snorted, a most indelicate sound for the elfin beauty. "Yes," she continued with a sigh, "in China, every piece of good land that can be cultivated is used to grow crops. Wheat in the north, rice in the south. Is it not the same in your—aiyaa!" Mei Li jumped back, and the two stumbled against each other.

A large dark figure crept toward them. It made tentative, hissing noises.

"It's a ghost," Mei Li froze, clutching her companion.

The figure emitted a low moan and stumbled on the path.

With Mei Li quivering behind her, Jackie had no choice but to handle the situation herself. "Mei Li! Stop digging your nails into my back!" she hissed over her shoulder.

Mei Li whimpered. "Oh, you have spoken my name! Now the ghost will follow me wherever I go!" She clutched Jackie even tighter.

Jackie faced the apparition with a resolve that belied her trembling knees.

Indeed it did not much resemble a human, crouching and waving its arms overhead. Its skin took on a sickly pale hue, and it crumpled to the ground whimpering and begging for mercy.

"Please …" it moaned, reaching out with one hand, the other clutching its ragged side. "Don't harm me. I'm nobody; a nothing."

"No!" Mei Li hissed. "It's a ruse! It wants to steal our ch'i—our energy!"

"Gimme a break," Jackie muttered, "there's no such thing as ghosts." Still, she gasped as the distorted face was thrust up against hers.

"What? Is it possible? Are you a foreign devil from the sea?" It peered closely at Jackie, and then the figure recoiled in shock. "Aiyaa! Skin the color of a fish belly! Disgusting!"

As her eyes adjusted to the early darkness, Jackie could see that this was no ghost before her, but a boy of about thirteen, and his face was not actually distorted so much as it was screwed up in curiosity and fear.

"Who are you calling ugly?" Jackie placed her hands squarely on her hips.

Mei Li stepped back in astonishment. "You can speak Chinese!"

The boy looked at her with contempt. "Of course I can, you beggar girl!"

Mei Li rolled her eyes. "No, no!" She pointed at Jackie, whose hands hand flown to her mouth in surprise. "Her!"

A loud clap of thunder sent them all scurrying. Thick droplets of warm rain drenched the girls in an instant as the young boy disappeared over the hill in a flash.

"Over there!" Mei Li pointed to a hut not two hundred meters ahead of them. A large tree hung over the thatched roof, bowed by the torrential onslaught. A stream ran furiously just behind the rough structure.

Jackie was doubtful, but Mei Li dashed ahead. "*Lai, lai!*" she shouted from the open doorway. "Come!"

Jackie barreled across the threshold a few seconds later. "Oh!" She nearly collided with Mei Li, who had been squinting through the rain for her. As Mei Li stepped aside, Jackie's foot connected with something solid.

"Agh!" Jon rolled away and jumped up in a flash.

The three teens screamed. Jackie and Mei Li clutched each other in fear.

Jon's expression turned to anger. "What—oh WHAT! What the heck is going on here!" he yelled at Jackie. He pointed an accusing finger at her. "I should be home now, in my own bed, not on some mud floor in a leaky hut"—he glanced at the water seeping in above them and his voice rose in frustration—"in … in … ancient China!"

In his anger, Jon seemed to take up the whole hut. "I just don't get it!" He slumped down suddenly and put his face between his hands. "And every time I see someone, they run away screaming. Like I'm some sort of ghost or something." He groaned. "It's all your fault. Well, your aunt's fault, anyway."

"To us, you are like ghosts," said Mei Li quietly. She turned to Jackie. "You know him? And he speaks Chinese, too? Forgive me, but I am confused."

"That makes two of us," said Jon, straightening up. "Wait, I really am speaking Chinese, aren't I?"

Jackie pulled out the book, which suddenly felt like it was burning a hole in her pocket. "It has something to do with this, I think." Her companions fell back with a gasp.

The book was glowing. Jackie swallowed her fear and tried to fumble with the clasp. It wouldn't budge.

"Hey, isn't that the book from your aunt's library?" Jon was stunned. "Or at least it reminds me of it …" He pushed a straggly lock of hair out of his eyes and angled for a better view. Mei Li looked at them with curiosity.

"Yes, that's it," Jackie responded quietly. "I can't explain it, but maybe because we both touched it that time …" Her voice trailed off. Jon nodded grimly.

"Anyway, for some reason, it's a conduit of sorts, in more ways than one." The two were quiet as they thought back on their bizarre journey through space and time. Jackie tugged at the buckle again.

"Let me give it a go." Jon grabbed the book from her shaky grasp. "Ow!" He dropped it and brought his hand to mouth. "It's burning hot!"

Jackie scooped the book up off the floor and wiped the dust off its worn cover. "This is likely our only way back," she snapped, tired and hungry. "So you better take it easy!" She glanced at Mei Li, now squatting in a corner of the small shelter. The Chinese girl had prepared a fire, and over a makeshift stove, was boiling water for tea. A thin stream of smoke drifted lazily out.

Soon, the unlikely trio had polished off some sticky rice balls from Mei Li's pack of possessions. Jon admired her resourcefulness and efficiency. "You would have made a great Boy Scout!" He sighed at her puzzled look. "Ah, never mind."

Jackie frowned. "You ate all your food so quickly!"

"I was hungry. What's your problem?" he snapped.

"You don't know anything about Chinese culture," Jackie muttered. "Barbarian."

Jon was astonished. "*You're* calling *me* names?" He snorted.

"Yes, Mr. Popular," Jackie snapped. "If that's what you mean." Suddenly, she felt emboldened now that they were in Ming China and not at Arborville High School, despite the fact that Jon had a reputation for being a nice guy. "Got a problem with that?" she challenged.

"Jeez, calm down," Jon said, "All I meant was—"

Jackie ignored him and turned to Mei Li, suddenly curious. "Mei Li, how did you get here? I mean, what are you doing here? I mean …" Jackie felt awkward for asking, but she couldn't get past the idea of a young Chinese girl traveling by herself.

"I should ask that of you, no?" Mei Li said quietly. "Why are two young foreigners wandering around my country? Unless, of course," she added, suddenly serious, "you are escaped slaves. You are quite exotic, after all. Did you come off a treasure ship?"

Jackie recoiled. Jon blanched. "No way!" he practically shouted. "Do we look like slaves to you!?"

Jackie sighed, thinking of their scraggly appearance. "Never mind. No, we are not slaves. What we are is lost, very, very, lost. And I'm looking for my father—and hopefully, my mother." She looked at Mei Li. "So, what's your story?" The Chinese girl sighed and looked down. Then she began, as if telling a fairytale:

"Once, in a grand home not very far from here, there lived the happiest girl in the world. Well, as happy as a girl could be on this earth." Mei Li's eyes brimmed at the memory. "She was but the child of a servant woman. However, the master's younger son took a fancy to her. As small children, they played together in the courtyard. When he began his studies—he had to memorize and recite important passages, and learn how to write with ink and brush—the young master shared his learning with her."

Mei Li paused. "This was not strictly forbidden, you know," she said, somewhat defensively. "There are some females who have had the good fortune of Acquiring a little education."

She looked thoughtfully at Jackie, who nodded encouragingly. Jackie clutched her satchel. Suddenly, Aunt Isobel's book seemed to weigh a ton.

"The girl and her family—her mother, father, and three older brothers—all lived in a small home about ten *li* from the master's family compound. Every day the girl and her mother would walk the ten *li* to Master's home, and her father and older brothers would head out to the fields to plant and harvest for Master. After the last meal of the day, the whole family would work together on a small plot outside their humble home. As you can see, I have rather large feet—though not quite as large as yours," she said, pointing at Jackie's toes. "That's how I know you must have been a servant or a slave—your feet have not been bound."

Jackie shuddered. She had read that in traditional China, from the end of the Tang dynasty until the twentieth century, girls as young as three had their feet bound so they might remain small. This was considered unattractive; a woman with large feet was unmarriageable in most families. Only the poorest girls let their feet grow to normal length, like Mei Li, so that they could work long, hard hours, usually in the fields.

"This went on for many years, as long as the girl could remember, until one day, Young Master was scolded by his tutor for sharing his knowledge with a female—and a servant girl at that. No one else dared reproach Young Master, as his elder brother Tsai Bo Wei had risen to become an important official. Their father had died, but thanks to Bo Wei, the Tsai family remained quite powerful. And because he was so remarkable, the light of his mother's eye, Young Master was used to making his own rules.

"He was very clever. He argued that when he taught the girl, he improved his own education, as he was forced to examine his learning. If he could teach an ignorant peasant *girl* such as myself,"—here Mei Li's voice cracked—"then he truly understood what he had learned. No one disagreed, as indeed the young master's studies had progressed at an extraordinary rate. Of course, that was because Young Master was truly brilliant."

Jon cupped his tea uncomfortably. It was still quite hot, and he was unsure whether he should put it down. He was still irritated at being called rude for finishing his meal. How was he supposed to know what was polite in Chinese culture—not to mention ancient Chinese culture? He blew on the tea, and the leaves swirled in a crazed pattern.

"Please continue," Jackie gently encouraged Mei Li. The Chinese teen looked up at the cloudy sky and drew a deep breath.

"One day," she went on, "one day, Young Master's tutor came shouting into the courtyard, where Young Master and I were chanting verses together. We were having a contest to see who knew the most *I Ching*—the ancient book of Chinese wisdom—passages by heart. Teacher ran in shouting and wringing his hands. The whole household was in uproar, and it seemed that the world was coming to an end, what with all the wailing and confusion.

"We soon discovered the cause of distress," Mei Li continued. "The previous month, the Emperor had sent a scroll from his own collection of calligraphy to each of the regional courthouses. This was meant as a generous gesture, so that he might secure the goodwill of powerful provincial leaders. Our own esteemed magistrate, who was the judge of our province and a mentor to Tsai Bo Wei, had received such a scroll and was to hang it in the courthouse. First, however, he had brought it to my master and his older brother so that they could examine it together. But while they were having tea that day, the scroll disappeared! Even worse, the Emperor's Chop was gone as well!"

Jackie whispered, "What's a chop?"

"It's a signature engraved in a round wooden stamp," Jon whispered back. Then he sat up straight, his interest piqued. "What was the Emperor's Chop doing outside the Forbidden City?"

"That was only temporary. And the Emperor has several chops, you know, but they are all constantly accounted for. You see, the Emperor's Chop is his seal, the proof of his authority. Any decree with that seal must be obeyed instantly and not questioned.

"Anyway, the Celestial Son had authorized one of his chief officials to validate the results of a civil service exam that would determine who would serve as an official at the provincial level. But now the seal was missing! Even worse, this occurred sometime during the scoring process! Who could tell which scholars had failed and which had passed? A new exam would have to be written, and the scholars might have to endure another three days of rigorous testing!

"I was sent off to work with my mother for the rest of the afternoon," a somber Mei Li continued. "One of the servants made fun of me as I scrubbed the court-yard with Mother. She reminded me that knowledge would not change my fate: I would always be a peasant and—even worse—a woman. No matter. We were dismissed early, and as we tried to leave, some terrifying officials entered the compound. We were told to get out, and then Master's house was turned upside down as everyone but us was instructed to look for the scroll and the seal. And that's not all; we were the only ones allowed to leave the compound.

"That night, the tax collector burst into our family home, with the tutor right behind him. The tutor cried out that I was the thief, a jealous girl who wished to steal the wisdom of the ages for herself!"

"But how could they accuse you so? Did they find the Emperor's Seal?" Jackie cried out.

Mei Li frowned and shook her head. "My mother was forced to hand me over to the tax collector. That was the last time I ever saw her again." She shut her eyes tight. "So I ran away rather than be his slave. Truly, all women were meant to eat bitterness."

Jon and Jackie exchanged puzzled glances. "OK, I get the importance of the Emperor's Seal. But what about his calligraphy?" Jon asked. "That I don't get. What's so valuable about someone's handwriting?"

Mei Li's jaw dropped. "It is a true measure of one's education!" She was shocked at his ignorance. "One can tell the writer's nature through his interpretation of *The Analects!*"

"*The Analects?*" Jackie did not bother to conceal her confusion either. "What are those?"

"Truly, you Westerners are full of ignorance!" Mei Li grew impatient. "Those are the sayings of the greatest sage of all times, Kong Fu Zi. My foreign friend used the word Confucius." She shook her head at her Western peers. Whatever was she to do with these foreign devils? "Kong Fu Zi wrote that the best way to restore order to chaos was to model proper behavior. There are five most important relationships in society, and these are in harmony in a truly civilized world."

"Oh, like you have to obey your parents, that kind of stuff?" Jon slurped the rest of his tea down.

Jackie gave him a strange look. Was he trying to show off? "So, Mei Li, what are those relationships? Please enlighten us." Jon snorted at her politeness.

"With pleasure," said Mei Li. "They are ruler-ruled; father-son; husband-wife; older brother-younger brother; and friend-friend. With the exception of friend-friend, these are all superior-inferior relationships."

"Hey now, I like that! Absolutely, men are superior!" Jon sat back triumphantly. "I've always known that, you know, in my gut."

Mei Li looked at him curiously. She nodded. "Yes, women are to follow men. But it is also up to the superior element to show the way, to model proper behavior or else,"—she paused—"or else, all will not be right in heaven." She stared miserably into her teacup, as if to divine the future in the tea leaves.

"Like what happened to you?" Jackie asked softly.

Mei Li nodded, staring at the ground. "Maybe this is all my fault. I haven't been submissive enough. Mother always said I never knew my place."

Jackie stood up and held out her hand. "You are exactly where you should be—for now," she said firmly. "Let's go. You have to find out what happened to the Emperor's Seal. And I have to find my father."

"And I have GOT to get out of here!" Jon thrust his teacup at Mei Li. "This is just too wild, man!" He turned to Jackie. "C'mon, Jackie, I've had enough! Where's that stupid book, anyway? I'll get us out of here, since you obviously can't!" He grabbed for her wrist, but Jackie was too quick for him. She twisted it sideways, turning her hand into a blade that she used to bring him to his knees.

"All right! Uncle, you freakin' ninja woman!"

Jackie did not let go. She put her many years of jujitsu training to good use and held him down with minimal effort. He bit his lip and turned white as she increased the pressure. "You won't try to touch the book again, right?" She leaned in menacingly.

Jon howled in pain. "All right! All right!"

Jackie released him abruptly and he clutched his wrist. "And remember," Jackie threatened, "I'm not a ninja. I do, however, have a black belt in jujitsu. That was just a gentle reminder to back off, you slacker tag-along!"

"Freak," Jon muttered.

Just then the skies opened. Mei Li surveyed the Westerners grimly. "You two had better learn to get along," she said. "It's likely to rain all night."

Jon threw himself down and claimed a corner. "Then I'm going to sleep," he announced and promptly nodded off. Jackie curled up a few feet away and stared up at the thatched roof of the hut. She never realized just how hard firmly packed dirt could be. She fingered the outline of the book, tucked away securely in her satchel. She clutched the bag closer as her mind raced through the events of the last few hours. *Hours?* she wondered. *Or has it been days … months … centuries?* Regardless, it was quite some time before she fell into a deep and dreamless sleep.

Truth uttered before its time is always dangerous.
Mencius

▼

CHAPTER 7

ALL THE WAY TO NIRVANA

The next day dawned bright and clear. Last night's storm had drummed out the unbearable humidity, at least for now. Jackie, Jon, and Mei Li arose early and after a scant breakfast of tea and noodles, the three packed up their meager possessions.

"Now what?" Jon wondered aloud, with a misery that Jackie felt.

Jackie felt warmth emanating from her middle; she had slept with Aunt Isobel's book bound tightly to her, for fear of having it disturbed. Three heads are better than one, she decided, and pulled it out. This time, she was able to work the clasp.

Jon backed up into a corner of the hut. "Oh, no, not again!" His eyes widened with fear. Then he moved menacingly toward Jackie, and his tone changed to anger. "Give me that darn thing! I'll get us out of here! After all you've done to me—" He reached for the text, but Jackie snatched it away.

The book had fallen open and Mei Li's eyes widened in disbelief as she squatted next to Jackie. "This book has magical powers," she whispered.

Indeed, the book glowed softly in Jackie's hands. There before them was a vivid map of China, with English and Chinese calligraphy dotting the landscape. In the upper left corner of the map was the inscription: Zhong-Guo. The Middle Kingdom, 1521. And there, marked clearly before them, was a list of central cities of the day: Xi'an, Nanjing, Fuzhou. And of course, the northern capital, Beijing, as well as the southern center of administration, from Tang times, Chang'an, the City of Heavenly Peace.

"Look!" Jon jabbed a finger at a bright red spot glowing on the map, near the southeastern coast of China. "Isn't that where we are?"

And then the book took on a life of its own.

Right before their eyes, the glowing spot evolved into a line that slowly snaked northward and away from the coast. It zigged and zagged, lingering longer in some spots than in others. Then it stopped, and the page ceased to glow, and the line looked as if it had always been there.

"I guess that's where we have to go ..." Jackie said dubiously.

Mei Li drew a sharp breath. "That is my hometown." She swallowed. "I can never return there." She shook her head sadly. "I am sorry, but we must part ways soon. At any rate," she continued, "with your book of magic, you have no need for a translator or guide. It is certain to show you the way home."

"Home?" Jon sputtered. "That town is not our home! We live across the ocean—and more than four hundred years from now!"

As Jackie continued to stare intently at the worn pages before her, she felt a soft tap on her shoulder.

"Excuse me, foreign miss. Did you lose this?"

The three teens jumped at the sound of a gentle voice behind them. A short, bald man in a simple robe smiled peacefully at them, and his face crinkled into a thousand folds as he did so. He was barefoot and carried a small satchel on his back. He also held a well-worn page in his hand.

"Please, do not be frightened. I have merely stopped to rest as I make my way to a holy shrine." Jackie and Jon stared at him, eyes agog. "This is a sanctuary, you know, for pilgrims such as myself. But of course any traveler is welcome to share this sacred space."

For the first time, Jackie noticed a small scattering of incense in the corner of the house. How many people had spent the night in prayer before continuing on to more holy ground? No wonder she had slept so well, she reflected.

Mei Li spoke first. "It's all right," she said. "He's peaceful. He's a Buddhist. Isn't that right, Old Sir?"

"Indeed. To wish harm against any living thing would violate the basic principles of my beliefs." He thrust out his hand. "Here. This is yours, I believe."

Jackie took the crumpled sheet and knelt on the ground. She opened the book on her lap and laid the sheet on the blank page on the left. It was instantly bonded to the book. She held her breath as the text began to radiate a familiar warmth. The once lost page, now opposite the map they had examined earlier, glowed with the impression of a scaly red and gold dragon.

"The imperial emblem!" Mei Li whispered in fear. "That's the Emperor's special symbol!"

"It is not wise to put emphasis on such worldly matters as possessions and station," said the monk, shaking out a thin blanket roll. He slipped off his worn sandals and sat down, cross-legged, wiggling his toes with pleasure. "Amazing," he mused, "how attached we are to our odd, helpless bodies. Our leaky, smelly, uncontrollable selves. Aiyaa! I have many thousands of *li* to go before I set eyes upon the shrine of the Holy One himself. Perhaps there I will find eternal solace and will not need to be reborn."

"Oh!" Mei Li drew a sharp breath, and Jackie turned back to the book.

There, just under the dragon, a small symbol began to emerge. The same symbol appeared on the original page, right where the red line had ended.

Jon frowned. "It looks like some sort of chop," he said, and touched the round symbol, which encased Chinese calligraphy.

Mei Li's eyes gleamed intensely. "The Emperor's Seal," she said in a hushed voice.

As they watched, the book ceased to glow, and after a moment, the pages fluttered shut.

Jackie fastened the clasp securely. "I was hoping the path would lead to my father, too." Still, she smiled bravely at her Chinese friend. "I guess we won't be parting ways so soon, after all."

The old monk still sat comfortably on the floor. "Ah, the journey may be long, but just follow the Middle Road. Then you will be exactly where you should be." He winked. "At any rate, that's what I tell myself, all the time. It helps." With that, he closed his eyes.

Jackie did a double take. How did he know about Aunt Isobel's instructions? She started to ask, but Mei Li put a finger to her lips. "Shh. He is seeking nirvana. Do not disturb him now."

And indeed, the monk was deep into his meditation, swaying and humming softly to himself. "*Amitobha ... Amitobha ...*" His eyes were shut fast against the earthly world as he searched for deeper meaning inside.

Jackie sighed. Just as she had feared, she would have to find this so-called Middle Road on her own. Why did everything have to be so difficult?

Jon gave her a playful punch on the shoulder. "C'mon, sport," he said. "Why don't we all find our way home?" Miserable though she was, Jackie smiled up at him.

And with that, the three teens made their way out into the countryside, this time with newfound determination and a spring in their steps. The storm had passed. They had the strange book of maps. They had each other. Somehow, someway, they were all going home.

Opportunities multiply as they are seized.
Sun Tzu

CHAPTER 8

▼

THE MEETING IN THE MARKETPLACE

Later that afternoon, Jackie, Jon and Mei Li headed toward a nearby town. At first, Jackie had been afraid they'd be caught, but her two companions had won her over. "We need information, and the best place to find out about your father is to visit a busy market-place. That is where everyone gossips," Mei Li had argued. "And maybe we will hear more about the Emperor's Seal," she added hopefully.

"And we need food," Jon insisted. "I don't know about you guys, but I need a square meal!" He cast an apologetic glance at Mei Li. "I know we don't have money, but ..."

"I will sell my services." Mei Li squared her chin stubbornly in a way that Jackie was beginning to recognize. "After all, that is how I have earned my cash so far." Mei Li gestured at the small string of knotted coins she wore around her neck.

Jackie and Jon looked at her, horrified.

"You mean you're going to ..." Jon could barely get the words out, and he reddened in embarrassment. Jackie could not look at the girl. Mei Li looked at them blankly, and then grinned widely. She brought her hands to her mouth in a futile attempt to stifle merry peals of laughter.

"No, no!" she giggled. "It's not what you think!" Her eyes twinkled with mirth. "I will sell my services as a letter-writer! You know, there are not too many people who can read and write. So people like me can always earn cash."

Jackie looked doubtful. "What if we're recognized as *waiguoren*, as foreigners? Remember what happened the last time? What if we get thrown in jail—or worse?" She willed her imagination to shut down. In the safety of Aunt Isobel's grand library, she had read of ancient tortures inflicted upon the Chinese: water torture, death by a hundred slices, live burial up to one's neck. She shuddered at the thought.

"You will wrap rags around your hair and cover your heads thus." Mei Li tugged the rice paddy hat down low on Jackie's head. As an afterthought, she picked up a handful of dust and smeared it on Jackie's fair cheeks.

"What the—" Jackie began to protest, but stopped when she saw Jon doing the same to himself. She shrugged.

"Hey, we have to play the part of overworked peasants," he said. "Anyway," Jon reminded her, "we have to follow the map. And the red line took us right through this small town." Jackie couldn't argue with him on that point.

Thus it was that three rather scruffy figures made their way into a nearby walled city.

"Guess there's no sneaking into this place?" Jackie arched a brow at the imposing entrance. A twenty-foot-high wall seemed to surround the entire town; she could barely make out the figures occupying the watchtowers above the main gate.

Mei Li nodded. "Even the simplest villages have some sort of protection, natural and man-made. To the west,"—she made a wide sweeping motion with her arm—"notice the mountains. Sleeping Dragon position. The back of the city is protected. And to the east"—she pointed in the opposite direction—"water. A lake. This town is guarded against barbarians."

"Like us, huh?" Jon asked. Mei Li cast him a scornful look.

"While it is true that you are ... that some people would consider you to be less-than-human, those we truly fear are northern invaders," she answered. "For centuries, feudal walls have held them back, but there have been times when those protections completely failed us."

"When was that?" Jon asked, his interest piqued.

"Once when the Mongol army of Kublai Khan overran our Great Wall, to the north. The Yuan dynasty that his people established held the Mandate of Heaven for nearly a century. We are now in the Ming dynasty, the time of brilliance. Our Confucian heritage, while not discouraged under the Yuan, is now more glorious than ever. The traditional examination system has been completely restored, and thus the most scholarly minds are chosen to advise the Emperor of the Middle Kingdom."

"Is that when Chinese scholars have to sit for three days and write complicated essays on Confucian classics? To prove their merit as government officials? To show that they are men of learning, character, and integrity? To ..."

Jon broke off and laughed at the two girls, who had stopped in their tracks and were staring at him, mouths agape. "C'mon, Jackie," he grinned. "Ya didn't think I was some dumb jock, didja? I know a little history. Remember, your aunt hired me as a tutor." His dark brows drew together in a fierce frown. "But that was ages ago—literally."

The trio fell silent as they approached the main entrance. The walls of the town rose menacingly before them.

"Wow," Jackie breathed, peeking out from under her straw-brimmed hat, "I thought walled cities only existed in medieval Europe." She quickly ducked her head as they passed through the main entrance, under the watchful eye of a fierce guard.

"*Kuai zou, kuai zou!*" he shouted, striking his spear into the dust. "Hurry up, you lowly dogs! Ha!" he spat, "you put your ancestors to shame, you worthless peasant mongrels!"

"Yeah, well, your momma," Jon muttered. Mei Li elbowed him sharply.

"Please forgive my brother." She bowed deeply as she backed away from the scowling man, dragging her friends along. "He is not well at all."

The guard grumbled and waved them along. "Simpletons," he muttered.

Jackie checked her anger and kept her head down. If he only knew …

She forgot her anger quickly, though, as they moved toward the marketplace in the heart of the little town.

She had never seen so many people packed into a space at once. "Wow, I thought malls were bad," she said to Jon, "but this is just nuts!"

The streets were so crowded that she could barely register the intense activity before her: here a peasant hawked his wares; there a coolie pushed on through, ferrying his rickshaw passenger. As she and her companions were swept along toward the market center, she heard and saw all types of things being sold: duck, rabbit, and goose vendors vied for space alongside merchants of ivory and silk. Jackie's mouth watered as they passed a wizened woman selling bowls of steaming soup and *baozi*, steamed dumplings filled with vegetables and pork. Crouched nearby, a man and his young son did a brisk trade in sticky rice wrapped in maize leaves. Mei Li pushed her way toward them, slung her pack on the ground, and began calling out for customers.

"Letters for sale!" she shouted. "Show your filial spirit by writing to your parents, who anxiously await your return! Plead with your ancestors for their divine intervention! Strengthen the family through ritual and tradition!"

Mei Li soon attracted a fine crowd, and with a grand flourish she took out a calligraphic brush and wet the fine horsehairs at the end with her tongue. Squatting, she shook out a small red silk cloth, as well as other tools of trade: an inkpot, a few sheets of curling rice paper, and her chop. Though she was dressed as a peasant, her confidence and manner of speech dispelled any questions. In spite of her slight form, with her hair tucked up into her wide brimmed hat she appeared to be like any other young man of the times.

"This aspiring scholar will write out your petition! Or even,"—she lowered her voice in a conspiratorial whisper—"or even help express your feelings to the one of your dreams!"

"Aiyaa!" An old woman leaned in and wagged a finger at Mei Li. "There is no room for such affection in this difficult world. Matchmaking is best left to the matchmakers, and not to young couples themselves. For shame!" she continued, revealing several missing teeth. "You are not worthy to be a scholar. May your ancestors see to that!"

"They already have," Mei Li muttered just under her breath. "For as a woman I will eat bitterness all my life." Her words were lost in the rush of the crowd, and just as well, for the sight of a woman wielding a scholarly pen in an open marketplace would have been far too shocking, punishable, even, by death.

To the old woman, however, Mei Li responded, "Thank you, Auntie. The wisdom of your years is greatly appreciated." And she gave a shallow bow to indicate her veneration of the elderly, but also the fact that a scholar was offering a token of respect for an old peasant woman. Somewhat mollified, but still complaining, the old woman sniffed and shuffled on.

Thus those wishing for a few written words, petitioners, merchants, fathers, and sons alike crowded in to buy Mei Li's services of the pen. While they jostled each other to be first, they were quite respectful of the would-be scholar's space.

Jackie and Jon, meanwhile, stood to the side, shielding Mei Li from the rest of the swarming crowd. "Clearly, mosh pits have nothing on Chinese marketplaces!" Jackie commented wryly.

"What do you know about mosh pits, mystery girl?" Jon laughed and gave her a shove.

Jackie returned his smile. "There's a lot you don't know about me," she grinned.

A middle-aged man in frayed, dark, padded jacket looked at them sharply. Jackie ducked her head, but the man continued to peer at her intently. In spite of the large crowd, he was familiar with most of the visitors to the market. While he failed to catch a proper glimpse of these two, he could tell by their manner that they were strangers to his village.

The man frowned; he had heard rumors of a stolen chop—the Emperor's very own! In fact, the son of one of his peasants had dared to enter his family compound a few days ago, dripping wet and shaking; he had been caught in a terrible thunderstorm. The boy babbled and carried on about two white ghosts he had seen roaming through his rice paddies. The man had him whipped, of course, for daring to enter the compound on his own, and for terrifying his three wives and favorite concubine.

Still, the man, a local government official, mused on the distressing news about the stolen seal. That the chop had gone missing was unthinkable, and the story was circulating throughout his busy town. The importance of the chop—a small, round, hand-carved stamp of the finest jade, with the characters written in the most exquisite of calligraphy—was not to be understated, and its loss was a sign that all was not well with the heavens. This was distressing, then, for all mortals in the Middle Kingdom. For one, the chop was a divine symbol, belonging to none other than the Son of Heaven himself. And another thing: this chop was in effect the Emperor's signature, used to stamp his approval or displeasure on the most important documents in the kingdom. It was not surprising that the reward for its return was quite high: no taxes for life, and a guarantee of one son's training and placement for government service. This was not only a most rewarding job on its own, but also a great honor for the family.

The local official was used to relying on his instincts to make decisions about the safety and upkeep of his town; he was also responsible for ensuring that no criminals were harbored within the city walls. Something about the peasant before him was not right. He trained his dark eyes on the slight figure before him.

Jackie felt, rather than saw, the man's probing look. She did not dare to raise her eyes to meet his gaze.

"*Dui bu qi*," she muttered as she squeezed by the merchant. "Excuse me." He grabbed her arm, but she used her jujitsu training to slip easily out of his grasp. She slipped into the crowd, looking back once to see him staring at his empty hand, dumbfounded.

Suddenly, Jackie heard a most familiar sound. Clear, sweet laughter cut across the marketplace. She would have recognized that sound anywhere.

"Aunt Isobel!" she exclaimed, and pushed through the noisy throng, leaving Jon farther behind.

"Oh, no. What under the Celestial Kingdom of whom the Emperor, the Son of Heaven, is the most filial son, oh what would have you believe that this poor book merchant has the knowledge you seek?" Jackie noticed a silk-clad man who bowed deeply before her aunt.

It was at this point that Aunt Isobel had thrown her head back in merriment. "Oh, please! You are the most renowned book merchant in the region! And"—she shook a dainty finger at him—"you have direct control of the largest printing presses south of the Yangtze River. You are a very important man, and your family has been widely venerated since the Xia emperor stayed the floodwaters of the mighty Huang He." Isobel smoothed her long silk gown. With a start, Jackie realized it was the very same Mandarin dress that her aunt had worn in her library on that fateful afternoon.

"You honor my family, but I am unworthy of such kind words." The merchant bowed more deeply.

Isobel arched a brow ever so slightly, and with a graceful gesture, pressed a small silk purse into the merchant's palm. "You are worthy of kind words, and so much more," she said in quiet but firm voice. "If you would be so kind as to tell me where this poor, helpless female foreigner might locate the source of the ancient text you sold to me, then this unworthy person, who may only look upon the wonders of the Celestial Kingdom in awe, would be ever so grateful."

Jackie marveled at her aunt's flowery speech. She had never known Aunt Isobel to be anything less than straightforward. Eccentric, yes. Grandiose, certainly. But there was always a point to her pronouncements.

Just at that moment, a small, thin young man hurried over to the merchant and hovered at his elbow with an anxious look. He touched the merchant's sleeve in trepidation.

"You worthless fool!" the merchant shouted, snatching away his sleeve. "As my chief assistant, you shame me with your mongrel-like behavior!" The merchant squinted scornfully at a fixed spot in the distance, never once deigning to look at his cowering accountant. "This had better be good, Li!" Just under his breath but loud enough so that nearby listeners could hear, he added, "Surely your scholarly ancestors are mourning your lack of decency!"

The young man trembled and bowed. "Yes, sir. I thank you for your kind interest in correcting my error-prone ways." He took a deep breath. "This lowly person begs your forgiveness, but a situation of the utmost gravity has arisen with regards to some merchandise that has …"

"Enough!" the scowling merchant barked, then smoothed his face to wish a cordial goodbye to Aunt Isobel, who had watched the whole drama without expression, her perfect posture a mark of her own good breeding.

"This lowly merchant must attend to trivial matters that his incompetent staff cannot handle." His voice silken now, the man bowed deeply before the foreigner dressed in the finest silk. He noted, and not for the first time, that this strange woman from the West knew the difference between quality silks, porcelains, and teas, unlike most other strange white people, who were happy to pay inflated prices for anything Chinese. He mused that she must be a powerful foreign devil; not only did she have command of plentiful resources, which were sure to fill his coffers, but also her people had let a woman interact in public affairs in her own right. She had appeared at his shop without warning this afternoon and had made most the unusual demands. Still, she showed the utmost respect and understanding for Chinese culture and tradition. He sighed at the strangeness of it all.

Aunt Isobel inclined her head gracefully. "This foolish woman from a faraway barbarian country is most thankful for any time your esteemed self can give her in the matter discussed."

The merchant hesitated, and then relented. He smoothed the front of his dark silken gown, and recalled the words of Kong Fu Zi, the great sage of the ages: "The gentleman is unhurried; the inferior man always acts in haste." He would honor Confucian tradition by living the words of this great master. He would not act hastily. Perhaps something was to be gained here. After all, the woman had showed proper respect to the most powerful kingdom under the heavens. "If you would be so kind as to grace my presence tomorrow morning for tea, perhaps we can resolve the situation," he said smoothly.

Aunt Isobel murmured a polite thanks, and the merchant bowed and walked back into his crowded shop of scrolls and texts, berating his nervous assistant for all to hear.

Aunt Isobel turned to find Jackie and Jon directly behind her, mouths agape. She smiled slightly, as if nothing were out of the ordinary, and then ushered them out of the main square into a nearby alley.

"I think we can talk now," she said, once they were out of view of the marketplace. She shook out a dainty parasol and lifted it high. "Jacqueline, take note: you must start now to protect your fair complexion. I'm glad to see you outfitted with the proper hat."

Jackie's hand flew to her broad-brimmed hat as she stared at her aunt with amazement. How could the woman even try to carry on a normal conversation under these circumstances?

Overwhelmed as she was, Jackie didn't even try to be civil. "You're joking, right?" Her voice rose. "Please tell me that you've gone completely out of your mind—" Jon laid a restraining hand on her arm.

"Tut, tut, that's no way to speak to your elders." Her aunt twirled her silken parasol.

"But—"

"I know what you're thinking, but no, this is not a dream," her aunt began firmly. "Nor is it a nightmare, for that matter. It just is. There is no real beginning, nor is there an ending; that much is up to you. Hmm ..." She frowned, finger tapping her lips. "I sound like a Daoist monk. 'That which can be named and is nameless'—Lao-tzu—Anyway," she continued, taking hasty note of Jackie's deepening scowl, "you may have come across your father recently, yes?"

Jackie's eyes filled with tears as she nodded. Jon put his arm around her for comfort.

Aunt Isobel took a deep breath. "Brace yourself, dear. Your father is alive. So is your mother."

Jackie's knees buckled, but Jon held her firm. "Ms. L'eroux, can you please explain what is going on here?" he said. "It's like we're trapped in some sick, twisted ... I don't know, some sort of labyrinth, not knowing what's going to jump out at us next!"

Aunt Isobel nodded. "I'll begin at the beginning."

Whoever can see through all fear will always be safe.
Lao-tzu

C H A P T E R   9

▼

"ONCE UPON A TIME, FAR, FAR AWAY ..."

Aunt Isobel fiddled nervously with the silken front clasps of her dress, smoothing the front of the gown. Jackie waited, her wide eyes threatening to spill over with tears. Jon coughed politely. The sun bore down on them relentlessly, but if they were aware of the heat, it didn't show. Finally, Jackie's aunt twirled her parasol, cleared her throat, and began:

"Your mother—my sister Judith—and I had, since childhood, been fascinated by books, particularly older texts, those rare finds hidden in the back of our father's used bookstore. Remember that place, Jacqueline? The Half-Moon? You visited once, before he was forced out of business. When you were a toddler, you'd positively dance with excitement when you'd see Tabby in the window, curled atop a pile of books."

"I remember." Jackie nodded, her eyes glistening. "And then that huge chain, Bargain Books'n'Bestsellers, forced Granddad to close the store when I was about eight. He couldn't compete on price, and he most certainly wasn't going to have cappuccinos made anywhere near his treasures!"

"No," Aunt Isobel chuckled. "'Books are sacred, to be revered, to be handled with respect ...'"

"'And not slurped over!'" Jackie laughed. "He was tough!"

"Well, that brings me to my point," said Aunt Isobel. "He dealt in unusual, and in some cases quite rare, books, but his door was open to anyone who wanted to learn. Children used to love to sit in the corner and leaf through his stock. Judith and I would spend whole summers begging to help. We just loved to hang around the place, and so did our friends. Dad never pressured anyone to buy; rather, he encouraged them to find their way."

"Wish I knew the guy," Jon chimed in. "I'm saving up for college so I can't buy books any time I feel like it. And it's almost impossible to check books out of our school library, there are so many rules!"

"What a shame," Aunt Isobel commented. She shook her head. "Anyway," she continued, "the summer I turned seventeen and your mother was fifteen we made a remarkable discovery. Father had received a mysterious crate containing three books.

"Now, people used to drop books off all the time, just to get rid of them: college kids moving out, estate sales, empty-nesters making room for future grandchildren. They'd just drop them off directly to Dad if the store was open or leave them in paper bags on the stoop if it wasn't. Our job, mine and Judith's, was to sift through the piles and separate them into categories: art history, science, poetry, and so on. Once a week, Dad would go through the piles we'd made in the back room, and decide which were keepers that he'd resell and which would go on the "For Free" cart outside his front door. Those were usually trashy novels, duplicates, or dog-eared copies."

"I remember that cart; people would go there first," Jackie interjected.

"Yes, and sometimes there would be a real gem. That was why it was so much fun," Aunt Isobel pointed out. "He just wanted to see who was really paying attention."

Jackie laughed. "That sounds like Granddad, all right."

"Then late one afternoon, this mysterious crate appeared. Out of thin air, we told ourselves later." Aunt Isobel's smiled faded. "There were strange markings on it, and we thought the writing was Arabic at first, but we turned out to be quite wrong. There was an odd, acrid smell to the box, almost as if it had been burned, but there were no scorch marks. Dad was busy with a professor up front, so we found a crowbar and pried the crate open."

Aunt Isobel fell silent, and Jackie thought that, for once, she actually seemed as small as she really was.

"There were three books in the crate altogether, all bound with a rich fabric, intricately patterned. None had titles, or any sort of writing on the cover. And then I picked up one and opened it." Aunt Isobel's eyes briefly clouded; then she shook herself back into the present.

"I think it's fair to say that a good book can transport us out of time and place, to another world, as it were. Some books have the power to change our lives completely; we can't imagine never having read them, and we can often pinpoint where we were, what our lives were like, when we picked up such a book.

"But these books ... the three of them, as we eventually came to see, all had the ability to literally take us to another place and time, in much the same way that you just experienced."

Jackie pushed the brim of her hat back so that she could look straight into her aunt's eyes. "But ... how could you ... how could you do this to me? I never wanted to go back in time ... although I would love to have my parents back ..." she faltered.

"Exactly," replied her aunt.

Her response puzzled Jon. "What do you mean?" he asked, crossing his arms.

Jackie glanced at him, suddenly noticing that Jon looked really cute in his peasant outfit. With his hair pushed under his hat, she was uncomfortably aware of his strong jawline and the way his dark eyebrows curved above his deep blue eyes.

She stared down at her dust-covered feet. "You know the man we met on the burning ship? The one we jumped overboard with?"

"Yeah, so?"

"That's my father."

Jon stared at her in shock. "But aren't both your parents ... well, you know. I heard they died in a car accident." His face scrunched up in confusion.

"So I was told," Jackie retorted. Then she turned back to her aunt. "Well?"

"Well,"—Aunt Isobel took a deep breath—"Judith and I would make these ... forays into the past, and always together. We both loved history and thanks to your grandfather's store we had plenty of access to the past. Art history and textbooks, not to mention semi-historical novels. Then the books in the crate came, and they sparked our interest in historical time travel."

"Yeah, I'm sure the History Channel people would have loved to get their hands on them!" Jon wryly observed.

Aunt Isobel nodded. "And others, too, others with less than savory motives." She breathed in deeply once more. "As you now know, the book acts as more than just a passport to other worlds; it's also a sort of universal translator that lets the reader fully understand and participate in past events. So here you are, children, speaking Chinese as if you were, indeed, living in Ming China, in the year 1521. To a certain extent, you ... blend, shall we say.

"At any rate," she continued, "Judith and I had a rule: always use the buddy system. We were never to go alone. And we were always to have a purpose, and a particular destination in mind. We learned our lesson the first time, when we found ourselves in the middle of the Roman Coliseum, about to be devoured by ravenous lions!" she chuckled.

"Not funny!" Jackie snapped. "How do we get out of here? And what about my parents? How do I get THEM out of here?"

"Yes, yes, I'm sorry." Aunt Isobel fidgeted with her parasol. "As it happened, your mother met a very handsome man named David Tempo, a young professor who specialized in Latin American history. You already know that they met in a history seminar at the university and they fell in love. And they married. And, with my permission, Judith shared the knowledge of these books, which were then safely hidden in my own growing library, with your father."

"My father would never misuse a book like this!" Jackie clenched her fists.

"No, absolutely not, dear." Aunt Isobel reached out to touch Jackie's shoulder. "But unfortunately, one of his students did."

Jackie and Jon fell silent. What next?

"Your father always had a soft spot for his students, and as you well know, would open his home to them," Aunt Isobel said.

Jackie nodded, remembering. "Our house was always filled with company, especially during the holidays. Dad would invite anyone who couldn't go home. He couldn't bear the thought of a lonely grad student hanging around campus, eating burgers for Thanksgiving. And they were all very nice to me. I felt like I had this huge family." Her eyes filled with tears.

"But there was one young man in particular—" her aunt started.

"I know exactly who. The history chair's nephew, Devon."

Aunt Isobel nodded. "What a waste of a human being. He inherited a fortune and spent his time frittering it away, always looking for the next thrill. His father, owner of a multinational company, was determined that he would eventually receive a degree, and he was equally determined to ... how shall I put it? ... to party the money away.

"By then, I had given David and Judith two of the books and I had the last one. Apparently he discovered them at one of your parents' famous potluck gatherings and lingered for a while after the others had left, trying to persuade your father to lend one to him. Your father tried to fend him off, saying that it was a piece of rubbish rescued from the Half-Moon. But Devon, cunning child that he was, managed to slip away with it."

Jackie's hand flew to her mouth. "I remember ... I remember my father panic-stricken over a missing student. That was the night we set out ... and the car crashed ..."

"Your parents called me right away," Isobel said grimly. "We decided to meet at my house and come up with a plan." Her voice softened. "Only they never made it. The car crashed and burst into flames. It was a miracle you were pulled out alive. And … their bodies were never recovered."

"Okay, I think I understand what happened," said Jon, trying to make sense of what he was hearing. "That guy—what's his name? Devon—took one of the books, and Jackie's parents used the second to go back in time after him."

"Wait," said Jackie. "We have the third book. Then how did you get here?" She looked at her aunt, puzzled.

"You're both right—but there is a piece that I've neglected to share with you."

The pair fell silent.

"The night of the crash, not only Jackie was found unharmed. Something else was recovered." Isobel gazed steadily at her niece. Jackie's scant freckles stood in sharp contrast to her pale face.

"The second book?" said Jon.

"It was found about a hundred feet from the car," said Aunt Isobel. "Police search and rescue dogs went wild when they found it. Amazingly, it was completely undamaged. The police were not surprised that it smelled of ashes; what confused them was its equally strong scent of jasmine and cedar."

"No!" Jackie wailed. "But then that means that my parents are lost somewhere and don't know how to come home!"

"Jacqueline! Shhhst!" Aunt Isobel gripped her niece's shoulder, glancing quickly at the alleyway entrance. No one was in sight. Still, she steered the teens a bit farther down the alley.

"Now," she continued grimly, "this is the situation. One: we don't exactly know how these books operate, except that they somehow divine the intentions of the reader. That is, one will take you to whatever time and place—within approximately fifty years and fifty miles—you are thinking about. Then it will lead you where you need to go. It is imperative that you stay on course. The book will ... ah ... remind you."

"But why did the book survive the crash? Why did I? What about my parents? How will they ever get out?"

Aunt Isobel held up a firm hand. "Clearly, they had thought about you right at the moment you were transported. They must have pushed you back into the twenty-first century and hurled the book after you."

Jackie bit her lip and then gave a small smile, as she thought of long, lazy summer days playing catch with her father. "Dad always did have a good arm."

"Ah ... yes ... I'm sure," Isobel responded slowly. "The thing is, I'm not sure what they were doing, why they were transported while driving to my house. The book needs to be activated, not only by thought, but by touch." She paused. "This brings me to my second point. You'll notice that we can all communicate in Chinese—because we all touched the book and we all have a connection to this place and time."

"I know what they were doing," Jackie replied, her voice barely above a whisper as she thought about her lost parents. It was all coming back now. "I remember. I was in the backseat; they were arguing about the book as we drove to your place. I reached over and picked up the book ... the last thing I remember is Mom screaming." Tears rolled down her cheeks.

Jon reached for her hand. "So what are YOU doing here?" he asked fiercely of Aunt Isobel.

"Searching for my family, of course," Isobel said softly, eyes downcast. She lifted her gaze to the bedraggled pair before her. "Quickly now, time is running out. This is what I know. One book has turned up in this province. I have heard stories of scholars disappearing most mysteriously. Judith and I always thought that if the intention of the reader is clouded or confused, the reader is transported, but the book is not. Now, Chinese culture is rife with superstition, so I'm not sure if this is really true. You know, there is always talk of angry ghosts causing mischief—especially unhappy family members who were not properly honored when they died. So this leads me to one conclusion: your father's student must have lost or sold the book. I'm not sure what has happened to him, but never mind; we'll leave him to his own destiny. For all we know, he might be wandering the countryside with us—or he might have disappeared to another time and place. That's his problem." Aunt Isobel's breath quickened. "However, my sources here have told me of a 'foreign devil' who was shipwrecked not far from here and has been earning his keep as an assistant to the local healer. Now that I know you two are all right, I intend to find my sister, David—and the stolen book. Hopefully, we'll get out of here safely and meet back home."

"But," Jackie said in a very small voice, "what about us?" She moved closer to Jon.

Aunt Isobel sighed. "By now, you must know that your particular journey back in time is not without purpose. While you are not to deviate from the path laid out before you in the book, for fear of disturbing the time-space continuum, and thus setting off an unimaginable sequence of events that would permanently alter history, you have a purpose here. There is something you must do. I can't help you in this matter."

She twirled her parasol and marched daintily out of the alley into the slowing bustle of the late-day marketplace.

"Whew," Jon said wryly, as he and Jackie watched Aunt Isobel disappear into the marketplace throng, "that's one tough lady."

"Look!" Mei Li waved Jackie and Jon over as they emerged from the alley. "Truly a scholar can earn his bread anywhere!"

The two were impressed at the business Mei Li had drummed up while they were talking to Aunt Isobel. Jackie was relieved to find that she wasn't annoyed at them for leaving her to handle the customers on her own.

"The local magistrate was a bit too curious about you, I thought," Mei Li noted, counting her cash and threading string through the coins. She gave a strong tug as she knotted them firmly in place. "Now we can purchase our dinner," she said, with not a little bit of satisfaction.

"Unfortunately, he was," Jackie agreed. Then she acknowledged her friend's success: "Congratulations; you're a real businesswoman!"

Mei Li looked up at her sharply. "That's not something to be proud of. Everyone knows merchants are like ticks that feast off the blood of their hosts. A merchant is solely interested in profits. That is not an honorable goal."

Daylight was waning, and the marketplace was emptying out. Jon helped Mei Li wrap up her bundles. "What's wrong with making a profit? That way you can buy what you need—and want."

"Pah!" Mei Li spat in disgust. "A true scholar is focused on acquiring knowledge, not on stealing money from hardworking people. Confucius had only disgust for the merchant who would profit from the honest sweat of others. Anyway," she continued, "I earned just enough to help us for a few days."

Jon looked at her strangely. "Well, where we come from, making money is the goal of most people. That's how people get ahead in life. Status is measured in wealth and possessions."

"Here in the Celestial Kingdom, status is measured in learning," Mei Li responded, her eyes wide at the thought of a nation of money-hungry people.

"But isn't it true that those who have learned well are rewarded by wealth, especially in the form of land? C'mon, aren't those who have passed the civil service examinations well taken care of?" Jon persisted.

Mei Li stiffened. "That is a different matter altogether. Their intentions are most honorable. They seek to best serve the Son of Heaven through their knowledge of the greatest sages, notably Confucius and

Mencius. Only the truly dedicated can pass those arduous examinations. They would never stoop to shop their talents in a common marketplace! What I did"—her voice turned scornful—"was out of strict necessity; a true scholar would never degrade himself so. There would be no need."

She slung her packs over her shoulder and impatiently motioned the two along. "Well? Which way are we headed now?"

By now, Jackie felt her aunt's book glowing in her pocket again. It was time, once more, to consult the strangest guidebook she'd ever read.

It is good to have companions when occasion arises, and it is good to be contented with whatever comes.
Buddha

▼

CHAPTER 10

THE CONCUBINE'S DISTRESS

Jackie unbuckled the book with a furtive gesture, and her friends shielded her from prying eyes. The pages fluttered to reveal a strange musical instrument. Jackie thought she could hear soft music, and a vision of a sad, beautiful woman beckoned to her. She put her fingers to her lips. "Shhh!" As the illusion faded, the red line on the map inched northward, beyond the city gates.

"Guess we have to leave now," Jackie said.

"That would be a good idea," Mei Li agreed, noting the rough laughter of the marketplace soldiers. One of them tripped an old peasant woman carrying a clutch of eggs. His friends laughed.

Meanwhile, Jon was rooted to the ground. "You're kidding," he whispered. "I don't believe it." He was pointing to something.

Jackie scowled at him. "What?" she whispered back harshly. "Cut it out, or we'll get caught!" She slapped his finger down, then followed his shocked stare.

There, in the far corner of the marketplace, was a very pretty woman teetering under the weight of packages piled precariously on her back. Something in the way she moved, however, indicated that more than her heavy burden was causing her distress. She gingerly made her way toward the northeastern gate, the crowd jostling all around her. She swayed, as delicate and fragile as a lily in a strong breeze.

An oblivious coolie nearly ran her down as he trotted by, a well-dressed mandarin in the seat of his wagon. The woman set her jaw, regained her balance and composure, and continued on her way.

Mei Li drew a sharp breath. "That is why I ran away from home!" she muttered angrily, and strode toward the distressed woman.

Jackie was confused. "What do you mean?" She hurried behind Mei Li. "You said your family was too poor to have your feet bound!"

Mei Li pursed her lips. "No," she said, "I have always been a stubborn girl. My mother said she should have killed me at infancy, as I was born in the Year of the Fire Horse—too independent for marriage and submission." She swallowed hard. "My sisters were married off, and each brought the family a decent bride price. But I was forced to work in the fields like a man. Except," her eyes filled with tears, "when I was allowed to help Young Master with his studies."

"I don't understand—" Jackie didn't know what to say.

"I set my feet free when I was five. I endured all my mother's beatings." Mei Li marched ahead.

Jon, however, was still frozen to the spot.

"C'mon!" Jackie doubled back and pulled him along. "Jeez, you're rude! Quit staring!"

As they reached Mei Li, she leaned toward the woman and said, "Older Sister, let us help you with your burdens." The woman glanced at them with a frown that dissolved as she took in the sorry sight of the earnest trio. Mindful of her light eyes, Jackie stared down at the ground. It was at this point that she realized the focus of Jon's shocked attention.

"My god," she murmured, "they can't be more than four inches long."

There, just under the tattered and dirty hem of the woman's brocade dress, were the tiniest shoes Jackie had ever seen. These, too, were made of brocade and were long worn out. Still, as the woman swayed before them, her shoes seemed impossibly light, almost elegant.

"Three-and-a-half inches." The woman spoke with a quiet dignity that cocooned her small audience from the rough crowd. They heard only her low, melodious voice. "My mother was very proud of her work. She began to bind my feet when I was but four years old." She turned to Mei Li. "Yes, thank you, Little Sister. I accept your help, *xiao meimei.*"

With that, the teenagers lifted the bundles off the woman's back and followed her toward the northeastern gate of the city, under the watchful eyes of fierce soldiers who waved their swords and shouted at the peasants not to linger.

From the corner of his eye, Jon noticed scuffling near the exit. He drew a sharp breath and stiffened. Two warriors were holding back the arms of a strong young peasant. A third yanked his head back by the hair and lifted a long razor that glinted in the late afternoon sunlight.

"Do not cross me, you lowly peasant!" The razor-wielding guard brought the blade down on the young man's exposed neck. The peasant stopped struggling.

"Do you dare to look me in the eye?" The peasant did not move. "Next time, I'll kill you and have my way with your woman!" The guards laughed and shoved their victim away. He staggered into the surrounding crowd. A thin trickle of blood streaked the side of his face.

One of the guards laughed harshly. "Ha! Who is next?" The crowd dispersed quickly, and with it, Jackie, Jon and their Chinese companions. They made their way out the gate without further incident.

For more than an hour, they trudged away from the walled city. Swarms of market-goers thronged around them for the first fifteen minutes or so; they shared the dirt road not only with all kinds of people, but also with chicken, ducks, pigs, and other edible animals.

"You're sweating!" Jackie touched Jon's sleeve.

"Shut up, Jackie!" Jon snatched his arm back. "Can you believe this crap? I hate you, I really do!"

Jackie stepped back, startled. She had never seen this side of Jon. Even though he was competitive in the class and in sports, he was known at school for being a laid-back, generous person—no small part of the reason why he was so popular. Jackie knew that he must have been seriously rattled, and she didn't blame him. She fell in silent step beside him.

Along the way, they helped a young boy and his mother push an obstinate pig home. The unhappy animal must have sensed that it was soon to become dinner, for it refused to budge a quarter mile outside the city walls.

"Move, you ungrateful animal!" the boy shouted. He hit the animal with a thin stick.

"Here." Jon picked up a rotten carrot that had been tossed from someone's parcel. "Try this." He fastened the carrot to the end of the stick and held it thus over the pig's nose. The animal snorted and started forward, angling for the carrot.

The boy grinned and grabbed the stick, copying Jon's moves. He flashed a smile back toward Jon and followed the pig down the road, his bony body a sharp contrast to the fleshy animal.

"*Xiexie*," said his mother, expressing her thanks. "Finally, we might eat soon …" She caught herself and looked down.

Jackie noticed the deep hollows beneath her cheekbones. The woman was painfully thin. How did she manage to walk, let alone look after a young son?

"Ah, your luck has changed. May the warmth of your ancestors continue to shine down upon you," said

Mei Li. She elbowed Jackie in the ribs. "Isn't that right, Younger Sister?"

Jackie bowed politely, desperately wishing that the book would reveal a way out of the current scenario. The woman with the bound feet arched a brow and said nothing, choosing to focus on the road ahead. The thin peasant woman smiled gratefully and hurried after her son.

*It does not matter how slowly you go
as long as you do not stop.*
Confucius

CHAPTER 11

—————————— ▼ ——————————

THE ART OF EATING BITTERNESS

"Please forgive this slow pace," said the elegant woman as the three teens adjusted their pace to match hers, slowed as it was by her crippled feet. "My home is just two *li* from the city gates, and we should be there shortly."

"One *li* is about a mile-and-a-half," Jon whispered to Jackie. "So this might take a while."

She glared at him. How could he be so smart? It hardly seemed possible that this shaggy-haired guy, now disguised as a sixteenth-century Chinese peasant, was once—or still was—one of the most popular kids at Arborville High. She wasn't sure how to feel about his company.

Eventually the group came upon a high terra cotta wall, its vast expanse broken only by a heavy wooden gate with a great brass knocker. The lovely and mysterious woman with bound feet lifted the knocker and rapped on the door three times. This was obviously her home. Jackie could only marvel at the incongruity of the dainty, crippled woman commanding an entrance to the forbidding structure.

The gate swung open, revealing a large courtyard paved with granite blocks. In each corner, a single strong tree snaked its way skyward, and the foliage from the four trees allowed only dappled light on the visitors. The very center of the courtyard was occupied by a short, square enclosure that was filled with earth and supported yet another tree. Far beyond the walls, Jackie could see the rugged Chinese landscape rising in the distance; the western mountains seemed to scrape the sky. She had never felt so small, yet so protected.

Inside the terra cotta walls, the air was significantly cooler. Though she couldn't quite put her finger on why, she felt lighter than she had in days. The mysterious woman seemed to sense her mood.

"Welcome. I am Xie Zhi Shan, and this is my home."

"We are honored, Miss Xie," Mei Li bowed.

"Please, call me by my given name, Zhi Shan," the beauty ordered with a smile. "You have helped me immensely. Now, you will all refresh yourselves in my bathhouse. Then," she continued, noting the foreign girl's relief as well as Jon's faint look of surprise, "I will share with you the information you have been seeking."

At this point, Jackie didn't know which sounded better. From one of the many doors that opened onto the courtyard, and old woman pushed aside a beaded curtain and called to the girls, curling an ancient finger as she beckoned. "*Lai, lai,*" she urged. "Come." From another open doorway, a hunched-over man called out to Jon.

"Later," Jon said over his shoulder to the girls who remained in the courtyard, still somewhat dazed by their surroundings. "C'mon, I thought all girls liked beauty treatments!"

Jackie rolled her eyes; Mei Li looked a bit puzzled. "Let's go." Jackie nudged her friend, and they walked toward the wizened, toothless woman, whose grin grew wider as they passed through the door.

"Ow!" Jackie flinched under the insistent pressure of the old woman's hands. She never thought anyone could have such strong fingers. The woman held Jackie in place with an iron grip, one hand pushing down on her shoulder while the other applied pressure throughout her body.

"Your ch'i is quite blocked," said the old woman, digging insistently into Jackie's left thigh. "We must release the blockage and thus restore harmony to your body. Aiyaa!" she chided, not unkindly. "You must relax! Stay still, so that I may complete my work."

From underneath a soft woven covering, Jackie groaned. How was she to relax when each jab of the woman's fingers pierced her like an instrument of medieval torture? As the woman worked her way up Jackie's body, each jab seemed to release pain, rather than energy, throughout her entire being.

The bathing experience had been much better. The old woman had stepped aside to reveal four large, scrubbed, slate tubs, separated by a four-foot wall for privacy. At the cluck of her tongue, three young girls came running in with wooden pails of steaming water that had been dipped from a large vat hung over a fire outside the room. Two tubs were quickly filled, and the old woman removed the girls' garments. She tsked over their bodily filth as well as the sorry condition of their clothing. Jackie and Mei Li mumbled their apologies, too embarrassed to look up at the old woman.

"Aiyaa!" she scolded. "I have seen goats and pigs ten times cleaner than you!" She eyed Jackie warily, as she had never seen a female foreign devil before, much less one with wild, tumbling red hair. Still, the old woman had seen enough in her lifetime to be surprised by much anymore.

Jackie slipped beneath the steaming water, her skin reddening from the heat. She was beginning to feel quite drowsy, when all at once two strong hands pulled her up. A young girl scrubbed her back and arms, then worked through her tangled hair.

"Funny, how it is like fire, but doesn't burn to the touch," she murmured as she scrubbed Jackie's scalp. Jackie slid lower in the water again and was left to drift until the old woman called her out.

Later, the two girls were turned out into the court-yard, dressed in simple but traditional Chinese robes. A cool breeze ruffled their hems. Jackie inhaled deeply, at peace for the first time in a long while. After the massage, she felt surprisingly relaxed and calm.

Far above the courtyard walls, the sky had deepened to a rich purple, and the dark mountains that loomed above them rose up to greet the emerging stars. Mei Li held out her hand and smiled. "Come, my long-nosed, pale foreign sister. Our benefactor wishes to speak with us." From one corner of the courtyard, a maidservant beckoned, and the teens followed, mindful of picking up their robes as they went deeper into the compound.

"Follow the sound of the lute," the maidservant said. She stepped aside and nodded toward a narrow corridor that was open on one side to the courtyard. The breeze carried a mournful melody that led the girls to a small room with very little furniture: three cushions, a chair, and a tiny table, with a woven mat underneath. On the chair sat their pretty guide from the marketplace, now wearing much richer attire than a few hours ago.

Their hostess had changed into a beautiful robe of the finest emerald silk, which complemented her luminous complexion. Her hair was piled and coiled magnificently on her head and decorated with pearls and jeweled combs. She wore tiny red slippers, silken and embroidered.

"She must be one of the Eight Immortals," Mei Li whispered into Jackie's ear. "The transformation is remarkable."

Indeed, while the woman's beauty had been evident enough in the marketplace, it was completely undeniable in these surreal surroundings. Gone was the dirty, tattered robe; gone were the spoilt slippers. Jackie wondered how it was that this refined young woman had gone to the marketplace herself to fetch necessities. Why had she not sent a maidservant?

Clean now, wet hair combed back, and dressed in a dark and heavy silken robe, Jon sat at the woman's miniature feet, his mouth slightly agape. The young beauty bowed over the lute, lips barely parted, swaying softly to the delicate music that flowed from her nimble fingers. The two girls remained rooted in the doorway as the lute whispered on of lives loved and lost, of honor and nobility, and of the sacrifice of following the moral road. Heroism was a double-edged sword, the lute told them; a valiant effort was always accompanied by great suffering and loss. The woman paled and her brow glistened as she plucked the strings, wordlessly telling her listeners of the futility of true love in an indifferent world.

Finally the young woman put aside her instrument and gently waved the girls in. "Please sit. May I offer you some tea?"

The three teens nodded, mute with fascination. The woman's long, delicate fingers fluttered above a small ceramic teapot, from which she poured jasmine tea with a grace that made it impossible not to watch. She passed out small, thimble-shaped teacups that were etched with the same delicate bamboo renderings as the teapot. Jackie hesitated, and brought the teacup to her lips after she saw her hostess do the same.

"It has been said that the Japanese—those from the land of the rising sun—have made an art of drinking tea in a special and complicated tea ceremony," the young lady said after taking a small sip.

"But this they learned from our Celestial Kingdom, during the Tang dynasty, when the princes of Japan were sent over to be educated by those who would receive them. That was nearly eight centuries ago," Mei Li blurted out. She blushed under the soft gaze of the beautiful musician. "Please forgive my impertinence." She sat on her rough hands and stared at the ground.

Their mysterious hostess smiled. "Indeed you are quite learned, Little Sister. Do not be ashamed." Then she offered pleasantries about the weather and the long journey from the marketplace, and she inquired as to their general health and comfort. The teens exchanged puzzled glances. Given the very strange circumstances of the past few days, how the two Chinese women could discuss such trivial matters was beyond Jackie's understanding. She gave a slight shrug in response to Jon's raised eyebrow.

Satisfied that they had made enough in the way of light conversation, the woman set her teacup down.

"You may wonder why you are here, and why I do not recoil at the sight of your pale flesh. Of course I know that you are not ghosts. You are people from a cold, faraway land." She rested her hands in her lap, and addressed the group like a teacher on the first day of school, outlining the situation, as well as her goals and expectations.

She spoke of how she was, at one time, the most favored concubine of the provincial tax collector, and how, when she was but fifteen years of age, he had first visited her hometown, known for its beautiful women and hardworking men. The day he laid eyes on her, and her delicate feet, he had decided that she would be his.

"However, he had three other wives, and to bring a commoner into the household would greatly disrupt the tenuous peace in which three wives, as well as his mother, lived at his family compound," the concubine explained.

"That sure is a lot of women," Jon muttered under his breath. "No wonder there were issues." Jackie gave him a sharp look, and he grinned.

The lovely young woman gave no indication that she had heard Jon's comments as she continued with her story.

"But this tax collector had arranged for me to come to his home as a concubine. This would placate the other women, as my lower status would be quite clear." Zhi Shan folded her hands. The teens were spellbound, but Jackie alone noticed how her knuckles whitened under the pressure.

"That must have been very difficult for you," she offered.

"Oh, no, I brought quite a high price for my family." Zhi Shan lifted her chin proudly. "As everyone knows," she reminded her listeners, "a woman is nothing but a burden to her parents." She ignored the gaping Americans and went on with the tale.

Her voice dropped when she described how back at his compound, to which she was carried for three days by canopied sedan, hoisted by four powerful men, the fighting between the women was fierce. A shadow passed over her lovely face as she recalled the vicious pecking order of the household. The tax collector's mother had been installed in the grand compound, and it was she who ruled over the entire household. After her, First Wife had all the best dresses and jewels, and was served next. She enjoyed a somewhat cordial relationship with her mother-in-law, as they came from the same clan. But her status was diminished by Second Wife's ability to produce four sons, one right after another. First Wife was barren. Third Wife was a pitiful creature who was broken by the incessant demands of the other two, as well as beatings administered by her mother-in-law.

"Before I came, they worked Third Wife day and night, constantly criticizing her every move. She would *pao lai pao qu*—run back and forth—in a futile attempt to please them. This was her duty as the lowest member of the familial household," Zhi Shan recalled sadly. "Third Wife suffered two miscarriages, and the tax collector's mother berated her incessantly for her unworthiness." Jackie gasped, and Mei Li paled.

"She hung herself two days after I entered the household," Zhi Shan said quietly. Thus the other women grew afraid of the newcomer, and demanded that she be thrown out into the street. They called her the Maker-of-Ghosts, and refused to share their meals with her.

"But I was his favorite, and am still," said the concubine softly, not without a trace of sadness. She told of how her patron had her installed in this bathhouse compound and would visit her when he passed through to oversee the tax collection. As his mother was keenly aware of his household finances, he had determined that Zhi Shan should run a business, and thus not act as a drain on his own income. "But he doesn't bother me with taxes," she added with a hint of a smile.

But as generous as the tax collector seemed, he had a dark side, as Zhi Shan explained. "Everything in this world has yin and yang, light and dark, male and female."

Jon didn't like the sound of that. "Don't worry, Jon, you're a totally manly man," Jackie whispered to him with a grin. He scowled.

As for the tax collector, the young woman continued, he had an ambition that was difficult to control. "His eldest son with Second Wife has sat for and failed the government civil service examinations three times. Though the tax collector had the boy's tutors beheaded, that has only worsened matters. Rather than studying hard to please his father, his son enjoys taunting his tutors with the prospect of a horrible death, should he fail."

"Didn't the boy's father know his kid was out of control?" Jon was shocked. He would have been grounded for life for such behavior.

"Oh no," said Zhi Shan. "The tax collector was never home long enough to witness anything but a great show of deference the young man exhibited toward all his superiors in the household, including his tutors. The minute his father left, he went back to his terrible ways."

The lovely Zhi Shan sighed and poured more tea for her guests.

"Forgive me for asking," Jon interjected, "but why are you telling us this?" He looked down quickly. Jackie noticed that he had reddened slightly.

Zhi Shan sipped her tea with a placid expression, but her hand trembled as she put the small teacup down. Her eyes darkened as she turned back the sleeves of her robe, one by one.

"My god," Jackie whispered. Jon inhaled sharply.

Zhi Shan let the sleeves drop, covering multiple bruises of various shades of purple. For a moment, it seemed as if she might cry. Then she looked up, clear-eyed.

"If it is my fate as a woman to eat bitterness, so be it," she said grimly. "But I have eaten much bitterness in my lifetime, and it is almost more than I can bear. The tax collector was reluctant to beat First Wife," she explained, "because her father was a prominent magistrate in a neighboring province. Although everyone knew that it was within his rights as a husband to do with her as he wished, the woman was her father's favorite, his youngest daughter. Second Wife was, surprisingly enough, close to his mother, whom he dared not cross."

"That's very unusual," said Mei Li.

Zhi Shan agreed and went on with her story. "In the last few months, the tax collector has been especially moody and quarrelsome with his formerly favored concubine, frustrated with his son's lack of success. He is worried that if the boy doesn't succeed, then everything he has worked for will come to naught. He will be deemed a failure."

"But—but—" Jon sputtered in anger. "In the first place, isn't he successful now? And in the second place, why does his kid need to pass some stupid civil service exam?"

With a nod from their hostess, Mei Li spoke up. "In our culture, wealth without rank means very little. The tax collector most likely was a merchant who bought this position and is good at funneling funds to the government."

"In other words, he's a thug," Jon said. He glanced at Zhi Shan's arms, which were covered now and once again appeared to be as delicate and graceful as the rest of her.

"Those who deal directly with matters of money are not considered to be persons of culture. Those who have demonstrated the learning and the wisdom that comes from years of studying Confucius and his followers are rewarded with social prestige, as well as a position in the government," Zhi Shan explained.

"But why would anyone want to be a civil servant?" Jon persisted. "Sounds boring to me."

In vain, the two Chinese women tried to suppress their astonishment. "Because," Mei Li responded in a shocked voice, "serving the Celestial Emperor of the Middle Kingdom is the greatest honor one could hope to achieve. By demonstrating a thorough understanding of the works of the great masters, especially Kong Fu Zi, one shows the moral fitness to assist in this most honored of all professions. Such success reflects upon the family as well, for this can only happen with the intervention of one's ancestors and living family."

"And thus one's *jia*—one's family, home, and all those living under one's roof, all those who have passed on, and all those who are yet to be born—one's *jia* is forever honored by the success of a family member who has passed the civil service examination," Zhi Shan finished.

"I guess it's something we're not used to, where we come from," Jackie said. "It's accepted that people make their own success, although their families sometimes help."

"Here in China, the individual is worthless. He is but a small part of the continuum that connects his ancestors and his descendants. Thus his actions are significant to the entire family," Mei Li explained.

"Got it." Jon nodded. "So—where do we come in?"

Zhi Shan looked at him evenly for a long moment.

"One of your kind, a pale person with colorless hair and eyes the shade of clear water, has stolen something of imperial importance. He has caused much disturbance in the larger towns, where he spends his days drinking and gambling. He does not respect the ways of our culture; he is loud and drinks too much. I know this because he stayed here not too long ago. He was very rude and demanding."

"Then why isn't he locked up or something?" Jon asked. "Someone should take care of him."

"Because the people fear his power. In the first place, he sold—for a vast amount of money, land, and servants—a mysterious book of magic," said Zhi Shan.

Jackie's heart thudded against her ribcage. Devon!

"In addition, he carries with him at all times a most significant and powerful item, which he uses to nullify all proceedings against him. Our local magistrate is helpless to initiate court proceedings against anyone who carries the Emperor's Seal."

Mei Li almost keeled over in shock. "But ... but I have been accused of stealing that very item!" Her mood quickly shifted to joy. "If this foreigner has the chop, then I am exonerated!" She turned to her friends, grasping their hands and smiling broadly for the first time since they met her. "I may return home to my family!"

Zhi Shan held up a cautionary hand. "Yes, I have heard of your tale of sorrow. However arduous the journey, I like to travel to the marketplace at least once a month, in disguise, so that I may hear firsthand, the real news of the province. However," she continued, "it seems that this foreign devil has powerful allies here."

"The tax collector!" Jackie gasped.

"Yes," his concubine replied with a knitted brow. "It seems that his son will finally pass the civil service exam. The Emperor himself will mark his approval—with his imperial chop selected for this very purpose."

Just then a breathless servant ran into the room, crying and wringing her hands.

"Mistress! Mistress!" The nervous girl trembled, her eyes wide with fear.

Instantly, Zhi Shan was transformed from a delicate flower to a woman of steel. She slapped the poor girl. "Calm yourself, wretch! What is it?" She held the servant's shoulders in her firm grasp, and stared at her, nose-to-nose.

"It's ... it's ... it's Old Mother," the girl babbled. "She's dying!"

Zhi Shan let out a strangled cry and ran out of the room as quickly as she could on her tiny bound feet.

Men's natures are alike;
it is their habits that set them apart.
Confucius

CHAPTER 12

▼

OLD MOTHER'S LAST BREATH

The three teens were momentarily stunned, and then Jon jumped to his feet. "We've got to—ow!" One of his legs had fallen asleep from being curled under him for so long, and he pitched forward. In spite of herself, Jackie let out a giggle. He glared back at her and headed for the doorway. "We've got to help her!"

The two girls rushed after him as he made his way down a long corridor that was open to the courtyard on their right.

"Wait!" Jackie called out. "Maybe we shouldn't butt in!" She hated nosing in where she shouldn't, and she had the feeling that they were in way, way over their heads.

"Too late now!" Jon snapped. Just ahead, they all caught a glimpse of Zhi Shan's robe as she rounded a corner and turned left.

They found her in a nearby room with large windows whose shutters had been thrown open to reveal a cluster of fragrant lemon trees just outside. She was kneeling by a simple pallet, bowed over the hands of a frail old woman who was an unnatural shade of gray. Spittle clustered in the corner of the woman's mouth, and she wheezed every breath. It was a painful sound.

Jackie narrowed her eyes. "It's the woman from the baths!"

Mei Li turned to her, horrified. Jackie was right. How was it that the old woman had been so vigorous and full of humor only two hours before? This woman was clearly dying, and at any moment, now.

"Oh, please don't leave me, Old Mother." Zhi Shan sobbed by her side. "For then I'll have no one."

"That's really her mother?" Jon asked. "I thought—"

Mei Li elbowed him. "Shh! Ignorant foreigner! She is called so out of love; it does not signify a family relationship."

The old woman lifted a hand with some effort, and slowly stroked Zhi Shan's glossy hair. She tried to speak, but no words escaped her lips. She fell back onto her pillow.

It was then that Jackie noticed the room's disarray. Drawers had been half pulled out of a large dresser, with assorted items tumbling out. A small footstool lay overturned in the corner of the spare room.

"Aiyaa!" A gaggle of frightened servants crowded the doorway, shoving to get a better view.

"Out! Get out!" Zhi Shan flew at them, and they scattered. She fell upon the bed, keening with grief.

Old Mother clutched a crumpled envelope in her hands, and with great effort, she waved it at Jackie.

"This is yours. I meant … to give it … to you." Her breathing was labored. "Take it. Now … before it is too late." She seemed to shrink into the bed, and then she was still.

Zhi Shan pressed her palms to her eyes, smearing her makeup in her misery. Then she drew a deep and ragged breath, and covered the woman who was more like family to her than her own blood kin.

She turned to Jackie. "What is it?" she asked in a small, sad voice. "Old Mother and I never kept secrets."

Jackie opened the envelope and began to read.

"Dearest Pumpkin ..." she began, and her voice faltered as she recognized the term of endearment that her parents had used for her since she was a child. She squeezed her eyes shut and willed herself to keep reading.

Dearest Pumpkin,

> *It seems hardly possible that you have found your way through time and space and are following, for part of the way, in my footsteps. Our paths have crossed once before, here in Ming China. Never thought you'd experience the sixteenth century, did you?*
>
> *Though I was determined not to let you go as we jumped off the burning caravel, fate loosened my grasp and set us each on our own path. I was comforted to learn that you are not alone in this strange journey.*
>
> *You may have already run into Aunt Isobel; if not, you will soon, and she will explain the mechanics of our time travel to the extent that she is able. She best understands how it works, at any rate. Your mother is here somewhere, too, and I will find her.*
>
> *You are to follow the path set out for you in Aunt Isobel's book. It is your destiny; it is the path that you share with your traveling companions. You must NOT deviate from it, or there will be dire consequences for us all. I don't just mean our small family. I mean mankind, pumpkin. If you stray from the*

book's marked path, you will change the course of history. I don't know why or how, but these books give us a view into the past, the opportunity to make things right—all without larger repercussions as long as we do not stray from the prescribed course.

It is unlikely that we can go back in time and prevent the terrible, huge losses: the travesty of the trans-Atlantic slave trade, the British concentration camps in South Africa during the Anglo-Boer War, and the Holocaust of Nazi Germany. But chances are that you are making a positive difference in the life of someone who now has the possibility to do much good, in his or her own special way ...

Mei Li smiled encouragingly at Jackie, who continued to read.

... and in this manner, the balance of world history might just tilt a little toward the positive. It just might.

So don't worry about me and your mother. We will be fine; I managed to glance at the book before I hurled it forward into the future with you the night of the accident. I managed to memorize part of our journey. We are meant to meet up again. We have a job to do. There is, in fact, something that must be undone, or else the consequences will be dire. You might remember Devon.

Jackie stopped reading for an instant. "Indeed, I do," she muttered angrily. She picked up the letter again.

Devon, one of my graduate students, made off with the last of three time-traveling books. I guess hard partying and rich living weren't exciting enough for him; he always seemed to need one more thrill, so he nosed his way to one of the books—and left. Perhaps because we were studying the silver trade in Ming China, he ended up here.

And so, my dearest Jacqueline, my beautiful, smart, and headstrong daughter, your mother and I must bring Devon—and the book—back to the twenty-first century.

Remember when your mother read our palms? That wintry evening seems so long ago, but apparently, to some extent, our lives have been predetermined. It's how we respond to events that complete the rest of the picture. Remember how we talked of Marcus Aurelius, fulfilling his imperial duties to Rome? Chin up, pumpkin. Believe it or not, this isn't half as bad as what he had to handle at the end of the Pax Romana. While he knew that his attempts to save Rome were only temporary, this most famous Stoic still carried on. He did what he had to do. You must do the same.

I have faith in your ability to find your way home.

See you in about four hundred years.
Love, Dad

Jackie looked up, eyes clouded. She missed her parents terribly. Still, she tried to shrug off her pain. "Ah, love how those Stoics always went about their work without complaint. But really—does life have to be so difficult?"

"Of course it does!" snapped Mei Li. "You're a woman!"

"You know, I'm getting awfully sick and tired of all these female-related complaints." Jon crossed his arms, scowling. His eyes flashed. "At this very moment, and for the last few days as a matter of fact, life has really, truly sucked for me, too!" He tilted his head. "What'd you mean by 'those Stoics'?"

"Stoicism, as a philosophy, developed during Hellenistic times, a legacy of Alexander the Great. Basically," Jackie explained, "it's the belief that responsibility and duty come first. Life is hard, and the challenge lies not in that truth, but in our own response to difficult situations."

"Yeah, I got that," Jon said impatiently, "I just find it interesting that you're quoting ancient philosophy!" He grinned suddenly.

"Right, because I'm such a moron in school, if that's what you mean," Jackie retorted. "You forget that I'm the daughter of a world-renowned history professor.

Believe it or not, we used to talk about stuff like this at home. That was before ..." Her voice trailed off.

"Chin up, eh?" Jon retorted. "You wanna know what I think about all this—"

A muffled sob interrupted his rant. Mei Li crossed the room and put a hand on Zhi Shan's shoulder. There seemed to be no question about it. Old Mother had crossed into another realm. Mei Li lit a stick of incense to soothe her spirit.

"Sister, what do you think has happened here?" asked Mei Li.

The concubine shook her head. "It is possible she knew of my plan"—her voice dropped to a whisper— "to rid myself of the tax collector forever." She turned to Mei Li. "Clearly, the foreigner who stayed with us most recently was your father. So we have had two foreign guests: the first was an insolent beast; the second was gentle and kind ... and he had bright hair like you." Zhi Shan nodded at Jackie. "He was a true gentleman. He had befriended Old Mother, and they spent many hours discussing history and healing. At any rate, all of our problems would have been solved, had our plan succeeded."

"Murder?" Mei Li gasped. Jackie and Jon blanched in horror.

"Murder, indeed!" A hate-filled, gravelly voice thundered from the door. It was the tax collector himself, dark eyes barely visible beneath his scraggly eyebrows and the fleshy folds of his face. His sparse goatee of long, coarse hairs quivered as he spoke. His dark robe did little to offset the paunch that strained it.

"Arrest her!" he barked at the four strong guards behind him. "Arrest all of them!"

A good traveler has no fixed plans,
and is not intent on arriving.

Lao-tzu

C H A P T E R   13

▼

PRISON PHILOSOPHY

"Don't look down!" Zhi Shan ordered as she and the three teens were marched through the dusty prison courtyard. Their hands were bound behind them; they were linked by a single rough rope. But it was too late. They had all seen the two moaning heads poking up from the dirt by the entrance of this house of misery. The tortured prisoners had been buried up to their necks and left to die in the heat of the midday sun. Flies gathered at their noses and mouths.

"W-what was that?" Jackie's stomach churned. She stumbled, and Jon thrust his shoulder toward her, as if he could reach out and steady her, but he was shoved by a guard.

"Move on, you foreign mongrel!" The guard raised a threatening hand. "Dog's breath!" He spat on the teenager. Jon was helpless to respond.

Soon enough, they were all unbound and thrown into two outdoor prison cells, cages of thick bamboo. Jackie and Jon were separated from their Chinese friends. Two guards—one fat and oily, the other as wiry as the first was fat—clustered around the pale foreigners.

"Look at this one—her hair is on fire!" The fat guard reached out to touch Jackie's auburn hair, which had come loose and tumbled over her shoulders. She slapped his hand away. "You must have had a very angry mother!" The two guards laughed.

"And her eyes! The color of grass in the summertime!" For some reason, this frightened the guards a bit, and they stepped back as she glared at them.

"Leave her alone!" Jon stepped protectively in front of his friend. The guards snickered.

"Does he call himself a man? With that hair?"

Jon reddened and pushed his shaggy dark hair from his eyes. He was too angry to respond. Not that it would have helped any.

"You're like a woman with her hair let down for the night"—Jon grabbed the bars of the bamboo cage in anger, and the guards laughed even harder—"or a monkey … no … a gorilla! Hey, gorilla! Your home is a tasty treat!" Jon gritted his teeth, seething with rage.

Eventually, the guards grew bored and wandered off in search of new amusement. They kicked dust in the faces of the two buried and moaning prisoners. "No worries! A few more hours and you will join your ancestors!" Surprisingly, they left Zhi Shan and Mei Li alone.

The day wore on. The buried prisoners fell silent. Jackie and Mei Li slumped against their bamboo jails, hungry and exhausted. Jon dozed off, and the prison courtyard was quiet but for his light snores.

"What are you doing?" Jackie asked Zhi Shan. She was sitting in lotus position, hands resting gracefully on her knees, palms up. Her eyes were heavy lidded, and she inhaled and exhaled through her nose. Even in such a squalid environment, she seemed remarkably at peace. She pushed back a stray hair, slowly opened her eyes, and gave Jackie a faint smile.

"I am meditating, my foreign sister." She folded her hands in her lap and took a deep breath.

"How can you be so relaxed? Here, of all places?" Jackie's own robe clung to her sweat-soaked body, but Xie Zhi Shan still looked nearly as fresh as she had earlier.

"I am relaxed. Here," replied the serene concubine. She touched the spot just under her navel. "In my center. Meditation is one of the keys to enlightenment, to nirvana. What happens to my body is unimportant. I can control only what happens to my spirit, by not straining against basic facts of earthly life."

"Such as …?" Jackie sat up straighter now and pressed her face against the bamboo bars.

"First and foremost, we must accept that all life is suffering," Zhi Shan began.

"I'm sure suffering now." Jon had roused himself. The concubine arched a delicate brow.

"The acceptance of suffering is the first of the four Noble Truths. Second, all suffering is caused by desire. Third, there is a way out. And the fourth Noble Truth is that the way out can be attained by following the Eightfold Path."

"Somehow, I don't think this is as simple as it sounds," said Jackie. "You're talking about Buddhism, right?"

"Indeed. You are right on both counts. This is Buddhist philosophy, and it is not simple. In fact, staying on the Eightfold Path is quite challenging."

"What's so hard about staying on some random path?" Jackie was becoming irritated, and she wiped the sweat from her brow.

Jon rolled his eyes. "Didn't you just study this in class?" He looked smug. "Oh, right, that's why your aunt hired me. To ... enlighten you." He laughed.

"Shut UP!" Jackie kicked him. Then she turned sheepishly to Zhi Shan, who was still in lotus position. "Somehow, I don't think I'll ever find this path you mentioned."

Zhi Shan smiled. "That is entirely up to you. For the path is not a physical entity. It consists of following the right speech, the right behavior, the right action, the right profession, and so on. But only you know what the eight 'rights' are—and this can only be achieved through deep and profound meditation."

Jackie thought a moment. "I see how that can be a challenge."

"Yes." Her Buddhist friend smiled. "But the reward is eternal: it is nirvana. Thus one can forever escape the cycle of birth and rebirth, and we may leave our weak and pitiful bodies; we may escape our physical form forever. We may leave this awful place."

"So you believe in reincarnation," Jon stated flatly. Zhi Shan nodded.

Mei Li had been listening thoughtfully throughout. "Pardon me, but some say that this is not a proper belief, as it is not Chinese. Why should a belief that has come from beyond the Gobi desert and TienShan Mountains be accepted in the Middle Kingdom?"

"Why indeed?" the concubine mused. "It was first introduced to China in the fourth century, but the efforts of missionaries Xuan Zang and Fa Xien helped to promote Buddhism during times of terrible ordeal and strife. Who would turn away from the promise of eternal salvation? As for me, I was brought up to believe ..." And thus the long afternoon was whiled away, with the four prisoners in bamboo cages thoughtfully discussing the meaning of life.

A stranger who encountered this scene—four live caged prisoners, two others dying from a most terrible form of torture, and guards keeping a lazy but watchful lookout as they awaited their next charges—would have surely thought the four had gone mad. But as it was, Jackie, Jon, Zhi Shan, and Mei Li were doing what many prisoners do under such terrible circumstances: they were staving off crippling anxiety and fear of a tortuous death by discussing possibilities beyond the physical realm. And as such, they were preparing themselves for the worst.

... give up pride ...
Buddha

CHAPTER 14

▼

ORDER IN THE COURT!

"On your knees! Bow down for the eminent magistrate!"

The small audience in the courtroom obeyed, but Jon was a fraction of a second too slow. A heavy foot on his back forced him to oblige.

"Eat dust, you stinking barbarian," the guard snarled. Jon came very close to doing so.

The four prisoners were front and center of the magistrate's high desk. The judge himself would preside over the courtroom for a few hours, perhaps render a verdict as well as a punishment, and then retire to his study to seek insight from the works of Mencius and Confucius.

Chinese magistrates were judges, powerbrokers, and arbiters of peace. As such, they were the glue that bound imperial China together. Since the reinstatement of the examination system during the Tang dynasty, all magistrates had to pass grueling exams that measured their understanding of Chinese culture and virtue. For about three days, test-takers were sequestered as they pored over the most complicated essay questions derived, in part, from the writings of Confucius and Mencius. Many only stopped writing complicated essays for a sip of tea, and some scholars even fainted from the strenuous mental exertion.

Success was attained by a select few who had not only studied and mastered the Chinese classics from a very tender age, but also by those who had passed the local exam first. While the examination system was offered to worthy candidates, the passing rate was less than five percent. This was to ensure that local government officials possessed truly virtuous characters and intentions.

Thus, to become a magistrate required years of study and service, the Emperor's approval, and the highest level of morality and dedication to order. This was because at all levels—local, provincial and imperial—government officials were to help the Emperor preserve the Mandate of Heaven. This would require moral conduct and action, for as Confucius had noted, "To put the world right in order, we must first put the nation in order; to put the nation in order, we must first put the family in order; to put the family in order, we must first cultivate our personal life; we must first set our hearts right." The Emperor himself, upon the recommendation of his advisors, the most scholarly in all of China, would use his chop—his imperial seal—to stamp his approval for groups of candidates hoping to serve as government officials.

On this particular day, however, the Emperor's official—the magistrate—strode into the courtroom with a confidence and arrogance that was most unbecoming to his station. The crowd parted as he made his way to the bench, and not a few fell back, shocked at the foreigner who was appointed to keep moral order and virtue in the county. Jackie refused to look up, hoping to calm her furiously beating heart. The pale young man smirked at the crowd which had no choice but to show respect for his station—especially since he was surrounded by armed guards. He made his way to the front of the courtroom, climbed up to his bench and crossed his arms, smiling coldly at the scene below him. Then he nodded to the guards.

"The disgraced prisoners, stains on our society, must all perform *ketou!*" the chief guard barked. "Down on your knees!" Immediately, Mei Li and Zhi Shan flung themselves lower and began knocking their foreheads on the hard dirt floor.

"What the ..." On her knees, Jackie felt a strong hand grab her shoulder from behind. Her black-belt training kicked in, and she instinctively brought her arm up and around, trapping the man's hand on her shoulder in the process. Then she reached up slightly, as if gathering energy from the air and drove her elbow down, like a spear. The guard cried out in pain and had no choice but to buckle to his knees his at her swift and sure movement.

The other guards laughed, and even the magistrate himself was mildly amused.

"That's quite a performance," he said in a familiar voice, clapping slowly. Shocked, Jackie looked up— and immediately recognized the man in the dark robe. This time, she sank to the ground of her own accord.

There, fully outfitted in magisterial majesty, was Devon, David Tempo's wayward graduate student. He grinned down at the four cowering prisoners.

"Well, now, what bottom dwellers are we trying to uplift today?" Arms crossed, he tucked his hands inside the sleeves of his magistrate's robe and sat back.

Jackie felt a surge of anger so intense that it roiled from the bottom of her toes to the roots of her hair. Even her fingers felt electric. How dare he presume to pass judgement on them? She shook with anger.

Jon's jaw dropped. "Wha—?"

Mei Li and Zhi Shan simply looked miserable. It didn't matter to them who sat on the magistrate's bench; they were prisoners, and as such, had no right to speak up or defend themselves. Devon was in charge.

"Remember me?" Devon smiled at Jackie with not a little trace of malevolence. He grinned to reveal very sharp, even, white teeth, clearly the product of the best orthodontics his fortune could buy. Why couldn't he be content to just enjoy his money?

Jackie purposely slowed her breathing and stared up at the thin blond man. Through clearing vision, she began to see him for who he was, an arrogant young Westerner encouraging misery for his own fun. His was not a happy countenance; though he was grinning, his lips stretched out coldly over his perfect teeth, and his face was pinched like a fox. Breathing more deeply still, Jackie gradually felt calmer; she'd found her center, just as she'd been taught by Zhi Shan. She was untouchable.

When Jackie did not react to his question, Devon repeated himself. Still eliciting no response, he cast a quick glance at the meanest-looking of the guards. In a flash, the guard pressed a meaty hand to the back of her neck, and Jackie's nose was a half inch from the dirt.

"Come, come, surely you remember me now?" Devon purred, one eyebrow arched as he studied the scroll before him. "Ah, so you have been brought up on charges of murder, yes?" He nodded to a heavyset figure in the corner of the small courtroom. There stood the tax collector, in all his vindictive glory, nodding back. "What a shame."

"A foreigner can not serve as judge in the Middle Kingdom!" Mei Li blurted. "Does no one understand that?" A guard stepped forward and threatened to silence her permanently.

Devon smiled wickedly. "Ah, but even a foreigner, if granted permission, may attempt to demonstrate his knowledge and prove his appreciation of the great Chinese classics. In this way he will be selected to serve the Celestial Emperor. While I possess a wealth of talent, I am not the only foreigner to succeed in passing the government exam. In the future, there will be a Jesuit priest, Matteo Ricci, who will pass the imperial exam; he will serve as a close advisor to the Qing Emperor. And by the way, you will be ruled by foreigners again, this time the Manchu."

The court gasped. How was it possible that this strange magistrate held the most alarming vision of the future?

"Nonsense! Don't listen to the imposter." All heads swiveled to the back of the room, where Aunt Isobel stood, clutching her parasol so that her knuckles turned white.

"Oh, I'm telling the truth. These guards here know that I can predict the future—especially when it comes to their gambling habits." The armed men scowled fiercely. "And now they owe their lives to me, of course."

Devon leaned back. "Of course, Ricci will be buried with full honors in Beijing—a distinction that he so richly deserved, given his deep learning and appreciation for the Chinese."

"Unlike you," Jon muttered.

Devon continued, unaware that anyone else had spoken. "At any rate, the Emperor himself has entrusted me with an item of the utmost importance." He removed a small object from within the folds of his dark robe.

It was the Emperor's Seal!

"Yes," Devon went on, rolling the priceless chop in his left hand, "it is my duty to act as the Emperor's agent. Thus it is that I will judge any situations, criminal or civil, the better to restore peace and harmony to our part of the world. In addition,"—he cast a sly glance at the tax collector—"I have the power to examine and approve any candidate's civil service examination."

The greedy tax collector nodded, and for the first time Jackie noticed the scornful young man at his side. He had something of Devon's malicious attitude, but he smiled politely. Then he rolled his eyes and spat on the ground. This must be the tax collector's son. Clearly, Devon was going to ensure his loyalty by approving the youth's exam. Jackie wanted to slap him.

"Let's see," Devon mused. "With whom shall we indulge ourselves first? Ah yes, the lovely concubine with a murderous heart. What a shame. Well, justice must be done in order to uphold the Mandate of Heaven." He licked his lips and leaned forward.

Mei Li lifted her chin and quoted, "Distant water cannot put out present fire." As Devon looked at her blankly, she exchanged a quick glance with Zhi Shan; the truth was about to be revealed. They both knew that there was only one reason why a scholar-official would fail to acknowledge the famous classical quote.

Without warning, a commotion erupted in the back of the courtroom. Devon's motley crew of magisterial guards fell back as a formal military retinue marched into the room. Leading the way was a tall young man, strong and handsome, with perfect posture. As he strode into the courtroom, Jackie noticed that he wore a dark robe similar to Devon's; clearly he was a high-ranking official. Though he must have spent thousands of hours poring over scholarly texts, he radiated an intense, athletic energy. The young magistrate was followed by a teen of noble bearing; the resemblance between the two was strong, and Jackie guessed that they were brothers. The official's eyes flashed as he confronted Devon.

"I am Tsai Bo Wei, the magistrate of the neighboring province, and I have come to assume control of your courtroom antics." He held a scroll firmly in hand. "Step down! By the order of the Celestial Emperor himself, he who possesses the Mandate of Heaven, I place you under arrest!" His guards moved toward Devon.

Devon smiled lazily. "On whose authority?" He picked up the Emperor's Seal. "Hmm, it seems to me that you are the one who should be imprisoned, for such a display of insolence!" Devon examined the chop casually. "It seems to me that my authority exceeds yours. Don't you know what this is?"

The young Chinese magistrate froze. "How did you come by the Emperor's Seal?"

"Why, he gave it to me, of course," Devon explained with mock gravity. "And only the most learned men of utmost virtue are ever permitted to be in his presence, the better to follow his imperial wishes!"

The young magistrate stared at the scroll he held, dumbfounded. Still, he stubbornly held his ground. "But this decree states that you are to be charged with trespassing, murder, and treason!"

Devon laughed, and rolled the chop in the cup of his right hand. "Perhaps those charges should be applied to you, my friend. Why don't we add the charge of forgery to the list, while we're at it. How dare you attempt to barge into my courtroom so rudely? Guards!"

Both sets of guards had been watching the verbal battle as if following a ping-pong match, heads turning from Devon to the real magistrate. The room was perfectly silent. Jackie held her breath.

"No! He's a liar and a thief!" a thin but clear voice rang out. "And he tried to kill me, too!"

Zhi Shan, crouched and trembling on the ground, widened her eyes in incredulity. There, walking slowly down the middle of the courtroom, was Old Mother, assisted by none other than Aunt Isobel!

"Thank you, *duibuqi*, excuse us." Aunt Isobel kept the gaping crowd at bay with her parasol. Old Mother moved forward, gritting her teeth with determination.

An audible gasp rippled through the room, for not only had a woman interrupted the judicial proceedings, she was escorted to the judge by a white woman of regal bearing. Jackie's eyes widened and she felt faint; she didn't know what to think anymore.

Old Mother stopped before the magistrate's bench and pointed an accusing finger at Devon. "You bring shame not only on your whole family, but on your entire people, you foreign barbarian! You devil from the sea!"

Devon feigned a yawn. "How regrettable. Now I have to kill you, too. And you're so … old, it's not like you'll even put up a good fight."

Mei Li could stand it no longer. "He's lying; he's no scholar!"

Once more, a shocked gasp ran through the courtroom. And then the tax collector's scornful voice resounded through the courtroom, sharp as a whip: "What would a woman know? Especially a peasant girl. Look at her disgustingly large feet!"

Isobel glared at him, blue eyes sparking with anger. "She certainly knows more than you, a lowly, corrupt thief who wished to advance his son through his lies and schemes."

The crowd responded, but this time in agreement with Aunt Isobel; the tax collector was known for his harsh methods, and more than a few suspected him of stealing the very funds he collected for the government.

Mei Li flushed and drew herself up tall. The frail teen was determined. She stared Devon in the eye.

"You have already proven that you are ignorant of the great sayings of Kong Fu Zi. You did not recognize his wisdom about distant water, did you? How is it, then, that you have come to hold this position under such false pretenses? Unless, of course, you stole the Emperor's Seal!" she shouted.

"Liar! You are the thief, you ignorant, worthless woman!" The tax collector hurled himself at her with lightning speed despite his bulk.

"Stop!" A clear voice rose above the others as the guards were pushed aside by Tsai Bo Wei's younger brother. "She is telling the truth! And she is not ignorant. Why ... she is far more educated than that ... that ... barbarian! She has proven it already, and many times over!" He reddened slightly, despite a remarkable control over his emotions.

Mei Li dropped to perform *ketou*. "Young Master!" He stopped her before she could properly knock her head on the ground.

Young Master Tsai held out his hand. "Please, none of that," he said softly. "You are my childhood friend."

The handsome Chinese magistrate smiled. "Is this the one you mentioned, Younger Brother? The girl who had been falsely accused of stealing the Emperor's Seal?" His sibling nodded.

"It's true, all true." Old Mother limped up to the real magistrate and tugged urgently at his sleeve. "I know for a fact that he stole the chop." She paused, slightly out of breath. Then she continued in a strong voice: "I was there when he did it!"

Shocked cries filled the courtroom. But not because of what she'd just said. Because of what had just happened.

Devon had vanished. All that was left of him was the magistrate's robe and hat.

The room smelled faintly of jasmine, sandalwood, and ashes.

"Fire!" someone shouted, and they all emptied out into the courtyard.

Muddy water, let stand becomes clear.

Lao-tzu

CHAPTER 15

▼

OLD MOTHER'S REVELATION

In no time at all, the entire courthouse burned to the ground. The central courtroom was open to the elements on all sides, and with a dry wind that had kicked up, the place was reduced to ashes before a bucket brigade could fully form.

But in an interesting development, the real district magistrate was found, along with his two main guards, bound and gagged in his own study, about a hundred yards from the courtroom. During the quiet exchange between Young Master and Mei Li, which the entire courtroom strained to hear, Jackie managed to steal away from the guards. As she crept out, she'd heard indignant, muffled cries from the nearby building and overcoming her fear, crept inside. There she found the three bound men, one of whom fainted at the sight of her pale face and red hair. Still, she unbound them quickly, and as she was doing so, the courtroom caught fire; the old magistrate and his one conscious guard ran outside at the commotion.

"*Aiyaa,*" Old Magistrate cried, "I should have consulted the geomancer for the proper location of my judicial bench! Surely the gods are angry with my carelessness!"

"No, most honorable magistrate," said Aunt Isobel, "the gods wanted to purify an area that was stained by evil." The old man smiled wanly; he was too shell-shocked to argue with this round-eye. Besides, she spoke with a strange authority; at this point, he was too exhausted to question her.

The survivors of the fire had gathered now in the old magistrate's study, interested in the latest turn of events. Even the tax collector, certain that he could curry favor with those now in charge, had hung around. However, his own menacing guards had disappeared in the confusion, as had his son.

When the weak old magistrate was given a sip of hot tea, he revived enough to pull out the lost scroll of the Emperor's calligraphy and explain what had happened. "At least I saved this from that evil barbarian." He sighed. Just a few days ago, Devon had arrived with two men of his own, and demanded to sit in the magistrate's chair. "He showed me the Emperor's Seal and claimed to be his personal representative. 'I always wanted to serve as judge and jury,' the barbarian said, and then went on to mutter that he was sick of being judged by others. Although he seemed quite learned, and carried with him a strange book of writings as well as the Emperor's Seal, I did not believe this man. When I protested, Devon had my guards and me confined in the most undignified manner." The magistrate shook a knowing finger. "It is possible for a foreigner to attain official status, but this is rare. And his manner was so uncouth, so unbecoming, that I thought this was hardly the case."

"No need to worry now, most honorable and good sir. I'll see to it that a new courthouse is constructed, one that will prove that you are indeed a man of integrity and high worth," Tsai Bo Wei vowed. The older man inclined his head.

"Me, too! Let me offer MY assistance!" an anxious voice cut in. "Why, I'll even collect extra taxes for you!" The tax collector raised his voice in excitement.

"The peasants—they can always be squeezed a bit more. They're used to it."

"Weren't you an accessory to the barbarian's ruse?" Tsai Bo Wei narrowed his eyes, and the tax collector, seeing no quarter, turned to run. He was caught not two steps later.

The threat of extreme torture encouraged him to confess the whole story.

"Not death by a thousand slices!" he cried, and Jackie felt briefly sorry for the man and his quivering chins. That feeling passed quickly, however, as he recounted the recent chain of events.

One day, as he was praying by his ancestral tablets, a great flash exploded near him, accompanied by a thunderous noise. "I had been praying that my eldest son would finally pass the civil service exam. Imagine my horror when I thought that this was the response of my long-dead ancestors!"

"I'm impressed with your show of filial piety," the young magistrate Tsai responded dryly.

"Yes, indeed," the tax collector said, nodding a bit too enthusiastically. Jackie felt disgusted. "At any rate, who should appear but the pale-haired barbarian! He looked a bit confused and was clutching the strangest book, all covered with foreign symbols and designs, the likes of which I've never seen before!" The tax collector panted in his rush to tell the story.

"Continue," the elder judge ordered.

"Yes, yes, venerable, most honorable and learned—"
The tax collector mopped his anxious, sweating brow
with the hem of his silken robe.

"Silence! Enough with the groveling! Just give us a
clear sequence of events!"

The tax collector started nervously at the harsh command and looked about to cry. "Yes, yes, of course!"
He bowed deeply and went on with his tale. "This foreigner had an air of authority and, as a good Confucian, I submitted to his will. He showed me that he
had the Emperor's Seal, and so by imperial decree, I
had to take care that his expenses and demands were
met. Why would a simple and humble man such as
myself argue with one so obviously powerful?"

"Because you had so much to gain!" Old Mother
shouted. "With the Emperor's Seal, he had the power
to approve the results of the next exam! And so you
beat my poor young mistress to compensate for your
foolish son's shortcomings!"

Zhi Shan lowered her head and clasped her hands as
if in prayer. She did not want to be reminded of her
unfortunate past.

Magistrate Tsai, noting Zhi Shan's loveliness and
grace, turned to the fat tax collector. "Finish the story,
you stinking mongrel's breath." His face was taut with
rage, his fists clenched.

"Well, I … I … of course I had my family's needs uppermost in mind, as would any loyal man!"

Old Mother reached up and slapped him. "What do you know about familial loyalty! Or honor to your country!" She turned to both magistrates. "Let me explain how the foreigner tried to murder me and how that man"—she pointed an accusing finger at the trembling tax collector—"how that man is an accomplice!"

Without hesitation, Old Mother described in vivid detail how she had happened upon Devon one night at the bathhouse. He had checked in as a paying customer a few days earlier, and the whole mood of the bathhouse darkened with his tyrannical demands for wine and gambling. He was asked to leave, but he took his time in doing so. She was passing by his quarters when she noticed a strange glow emanating from his room, and peeked in.

"The door was part open," she explained. "I'm really not that nosy, you know."

The young magistrate patted her hand. "We understand, Old Mother."

Zhi Shan cast him a lovely, grateful smile, which he returned in full.

Old Mother continued with her story: she had seen the book begin to tremble beneath Devon's hands, and strange symbols and a path seemed to leap up at him.

"Then I heard him say, 'Aha ... so the Emperor's Seal is the key to the Celestial Kingdom.' And suddenly we were both in the Forbidden City, in his Celestial Majesty's study. I was so frightened, for it is a curse to set foot where one does not belong! There, on the Emperor's elegant teak writing table, was his chop. The barbarian grabbed it and in an instant we both were back in his quarters. I was shaking like a leaf. He made me promise not to reveal what I'd seen."

"So that's why he tried to kill you," Jackie said quietly. "Devon stole the Emperor's Seal—and you were the witness!"

"As was I," revealed Mei Li. All eyes fixed on her, and she stared straight down.

Jackie stared at her friend. "How is that possible? I thought—"

"I had heard of the Emperor's extensive collection of maps and books. I wanted to see for myself. I ... I know what I did was wrong, but I didn't touch anything; to simply behold the vast treasure of learning was enough. When Devon saw me there, crouched among the scrolls, he was very, very angry."

"Naturally, but for all the wrong reasons. As a peasant woman, as an outsider to the Forbidden City, your presence is punishable by death, you know," the young magistrate said coldly, suddenly authoritative. His younger brother let out a cry. "I'm sorry, but that's the law."

"Hasn't she suffered enough?" his younger brother said in a choked voice. "She was separated from her family … and friends …" He struggled to regain his composure. "And it's my fault, anyway, for encouraging her intellect."

"But this explains why she was accused of stealing the emperor's chop——she knew the truth!"

"And who would believe a peasant girl, anyway?" Mei Li added softly, not daring to raise her eyes. Jackie reached out and squeezed her hand. Mei Li smiled bravely.

"Yes, and your father knew of all this." Old Mother nodded at Jackie. "He was trying to track down that Devon, so as to stop his evildoing! He saw that we would cross paths, and that is why he left you the letter." Jackie's throat felt tight. "My," Old Mother observed, "the books your people possess are powerful indeed."

"Indeed. We must also consider that there are times when the reed must bend so that it doesn't break under the force of the wind." The older magistrate smiled. "Let us bend here. The young lady … both young ladies"—he nodded to Zhi Shan—"have suffered enough." He fixed on the tax collector. "But as for you, you worthless fool," he said coldly, "the barbarian Devon did not possess the Emperor's Seal: you told him of its power, and promised him all the riches he desired should he procure it for your son. Yes indeed, your suffering is yet to come."

And with that, the guards pulled the wailing man out of the room.

Wheresoever you go, go with all your heart.
Confucius

CHAPTER 16

▼

THE LAST SUPPER

Later, they convened at the bathhouse to celebrate. Old Magistrate had returned to his family compound, where he was joyfully reunited with his three wives, twelve children, and sixteen grandchildren. Thus it was that Jackie, Jon, Aunt Isobel, Mei Li, the concubine Zhi Shan, the handsome Tsai Bo Wei, and his younger brother sat for a long and jovial meal. Old Mother had refused to sit with them, laughing, "It is not my place! And anyway, I have work to do!" She accepted a cup of hot jasmine tea, then hobbled out to the bathhouse, grumbling happily about its state of neglect since her sickness and absence. "Aiyaa! I pray that the gods send me some decent help!" The remaining guests laughed.

Dish after dish appeared. "Please, you must have this." Mei Li offered a fish eyeball to Jackie, who shrieked loudly.

The Chinese teen was shocked by Jackie's response. The eyeball quivered in her chopsticks. "But this is the most delicate part. I offer it to you out of friendship!"

"Yeah, Jackie." Jon grinned. "Eat it!"

Jackie took a deep breath. "Yes, thank you for your unending generosity. I could not help but shout for joy, but I cannot accept this gift. Please, let us remember how helpful Jon was during terrible times of travail." She turned to Jon, a mischievous smile on her lips.

Mei Li insisted that he take the eyeball. Jon blanched and choked it down.

"I am honored," he croaked. Jackie could barely contain her giggles.

An hour later, Jon was till trying to keep up with the food. "When are the dishes going to stop coming out?" he groaned.

"When you stop eating," said the concubine with a gentle smile. "Please, have some more. As much as you like."

Jon noticed that the others were grinning at him and realized that they had put down their chopsticks long ago. "Oh," he said stupidly. "I was always taught to clean my plate."

His Chinese friends laughed and explained that their custom was to feed a visitor until he swore he was sated and left some food on his plate to show that he could not force down another mouthful. Until then, his hosts were obliged to continue plying him with food.

"Oops," Jon burped. "I reached that point half an hour ago."

And so it went. The evening passed amidst much laughter and food. Aunt Isobel enthralled them with fanciful tales of faraway lands. Zhi Shan called for her lute and played songs of hope and joy. The music filled the entire compound, lifting the hearts of her listeners with every melodic pluck.

Later, the young magistrate drew Zhi Shan into a private conversation. "The tax collector is in jail, and he is likely to serve a long sentence."

Zhi Shan sighed with relief.

The young man put a finger under her chin and gently lifted her face toward his. She stiffened.

"I have been consumed with work and until today have not lifted my head to take in the beauty before me. Please," he said softly, "you are a free woman now. Would you consider becoming my wife?"

Zhi Shan nodded slowly, a single tear creeping down her beautiful face. "But I am most unworthy."

"Not to me," said the young magistrate.

He promised to visit her tomorrow. "You should start packing for the journey to your new home. The bride sedan will come for you and all your belongings in three days' time. Remember, you will never return to this place." Nodding to his grinning younger brother, he added, "Yes, of course Mei Li will come home with us as well!" The young men left.

"So you shall be my sister!" Zhi Shan sang. The two young women clutched each other for joy, and Old Mother had been listening at the door; now she ran to them, clapping her hands.

"Aiyaa! Aiyaa! Your fortune has finally changed!" She did a little dance and held them close.

As she grinned at the giddy celebration before them, Jackie suddenly realized how tired she was. "I think I'm going to turn in now," she said to Jon, who was still rubbing his stomach ruefully.

"Me, too," he agreed—and burped again. Jackie laughed and shook her head.

Then she felt a familiar burning sensation: the book was trying to tell her something. She pulled it out slowly in half dread, and the pages fluttered open to the map of China. There was very little space ahead of the glowing red line.

Jackie squinted. "I think we're supposed to get a move on, but it doesn't show where we're supposed to go."

"Yeah, yeah. Just follow the Middle Road," Jon said.

"I think it's high time that you followed your feet to bed." Aunt Isobel said firmly, and steered to the two toward the door. "Come, now. It's time to rest. We still have a long way to go."

Jackie showed her the book. "Hmm, we may be on our way tonight, after all," Isobel said thoughtfully.

They thanked their hostess and said goodnight to all. The courtyard seemed to be lit by a thousand bright stars. The moon hung heavy and bright in the purple evening sky.

"Do you think we've done the right thing?" Jackie asked as they inhaled the crisp evening air. Jon put his arm around her, ignoring Aunt Isobel's raised eyebrow, and they all started across the courtyard together.

"Well, let's see. You tried to find your parents, and you know now that they're safe. Directly or indirectly, you helped two women with otherwise very unfortunate lives. Their path seems much happier now, at least to me."

"Yeah," Jackie said. "Maybe." Then she pointed to an oddly lit arched doorway. "I think that's where we're supposed to go. See, the line ends there." She pointed at a page in the glowing book.

Jon looked down at his feet. "Anyway, let's follow this interesting path."

"Okay," Jackie agreed. Her aunt seemed to hesitate. "Coming, Aunt Isobel? Isn't that the way …?"

The older woman smiled, and it seemed to Jackie that she had never seen her aunt look so tired.

"Yes, dear." Aunt Isobel reached for her niece's hand.

As they drew closer, the doorway glowed with a strange intensity. Instinctively, Jackie reached for her book but it was too late.

They crossed the threshold into nothingness.

*For the wise man looks into space
and he knows there are no limited dimensions.*
Confucius

CHAPTER 17

BACK TO THE FUTURE

"Ugh. Stop. Stop!"

Halfway around the world and some four hundred years later, the teens found themselves on the floor of Aunt Isobel's library. Jackie's face felt like it was being sanded by Wolfe's rough tongue.

"Wolfe!" she shrieked and threw her arms around the happy dog. "You brute!" He barked and jumped up on her. She laughed, reveling in the moment.

The terrible storm had abated. Sunlight sparkled on a fresh new world outside.

Jackie grinned at Jon, who sat dazed on the thick Persian rug. "C'mon." She grinned and offered her hand. "Don't you have a job to do?" He grinned back and unfolded himself, stretching to his full height. "You tell me." "Well," she said, "I guess we could always follow that Middle Road." "Indeed!" Aunt Isobel appeared, shaking out her parasol. "And that includes writing your term paper!"

Everything was the same, yet all had changed. Somewhere far away, in another time and place, Jackie's parents had finally found each other. David and Judith Tempo had some time, for now, to linger in each other's company. They were content in the knowledge revealed to them through their book: that their daughter was safe. That given the circumstances, she was as happy as she could be. And that someday, somehow, they would all be together again.

Aunt Isobel's book, safely tucked in an uppermost shelf in the library, gave off an eerie light in the dark. Halfway across the house, Wolfe lifted his head off his paws and pricked up his ears. Then he thrust his head down again, whining softly. He burrowed closer to a sleeping Jackie, who clutched her covers tightly to her chest. Her eyes opened slightly in the dark, and it seemed to Wolfe that she, too, had heard the faint rhythm of African drums, and the war cries that accompanied the insistent music. But Jackie's eyes fluttered shut again, as she sank deeper into her dreams of times past—and of times yet to come.

THE END

978-0-595-46822-5
0-595-46822-5

Printed in the United States
203062BV00002B/1-48/A

9 780595 468225